FROM THE
NANCY DREW FILES

THE CASE: The Razor's Edge dance club—it's the place to be . . . for kidnapping and murder!

CONTACT: When Bess asked Nancy to come down to the club, she had no idea it would be an invitation to her own disappearance.

SUSPECTS: Charity Freeborn—Bess took her job at the Razor's Edge . . . and now Charity may have taken revenge.

Tom Kragen—A photographer whose open interest in Bess may have turned into a secret obsession.

Gaetan Orakuma—His bad business dealings with the club DJ may have led to bad blood.

COMPLICATIONS: DJ Etienne Girard clearly had a hand in the kidnapping—a fact Nancy learns too late . . . after the discovery of his body.

Books in The Nancy Drew Files® Series

Available from ARCHWAY Paperbacks

The NANCY DREW

Files™
100

DANCE TILL YOU DIE

CAROLYN KEENE

AN ARCHWAY PAPERBACK
Published by POCKET BOOKS
New York   London   Toronto   Sydney   Tokyo   Singapore

AN ARCHWAY PAPERBACK *Original*

An Archway Paperback published by
POCKET BOOKS, a division of Simon & Schuster Inc.
1230 Avenue of the Americas, New York, NY 10020

Copyright © 1994 by Simon & Schuster Inc.
Produced by Mega-Books of New York, Inc.

ISBN: 0-671-79492-2

First Archway Paperback printing October 1994

10 9 8 7 6 5 4 3 2 1

NANCY DREW, AN ARCHWAY PAPERBACK and colophon are registered trademarks of Simon & Schuster Inc.

THE NANCY DREW FILES is a trademark of Simon & Schuster Inc.

Cover art by Cliff Miller

Printed in the U.S.A.

IL 6+

DANCE TILL YOU DIE

Chapter

One

SHORTS AND T-SHIRTS in October? George, we *must* be out of our minds!" Laughing, Nancy Drew turned to her friend and held up a blue-and-white top. "Do you think this top and these shorts will be right for tonight?"

George Fayne shook her head in mock dismay as she eyed Nancy's lightweight clothes. "I know tonight's dance at the club has a beach theme, but I'm wearing a heavy coat."

"Good idea," Nancy agreed. The entirety of Nancy's summer wardrobe was strewn across her bedroom. She pulled the gauzy blue-and-white midriff blouse over her head and slipped into a pair of denim cutoffs. George was already wearing her outfit for the evening, a cute white tennis dress with a flared skirt. "I can't wait to see what Bess will be wearing for her debut at the Razor's Edge," Nancy continued. "She's been keeping me in suspense all week."

The Razor's Edge was a popular teen dance club in River Heights. Nancy's friend and George's cousin, Bess Marvin, was going to start a new job there that night.

"Speaking of suspense," George said as she smoothed the pleats on her skirt, "I don't know what kind of job Bess has at the club. She's been very mysterious about the whole thing."

"Well, I can solve that mystery. She's a theme hostess, which means she organizes and dresses up in costumes for special theme parties. Like tonight's beach night," Nancy explained. She dropped onto a little padded stool in front of her dressing table and ran a brush through her thick strawberry blond hair. "She must have come up with quite an outfit, to keep it a secret all week."

"They're actually paying her to stand around in a costume all night?" George sounded disbelieving. "Only Bess could land a job like that," she added with a mischievous grin. "How did she land that job, anyway?"

"I think she answered an ad in the paper."

Nancy glanced at her watch. "Oops, it's almost eight o'clock. We'd better get going."

The two friends left Nancy's bedroom and headed downstairs. In the front hall they met Hannah Gruen, the Drews' housekeeper. " 'Bye, Hannah." Nancy gave Hannah a quick hug. "Just pretend you don't see how messy my room is—I'll pick it up when I come home!"

"I'll put blinders on till you get back," Hannah joked. The cheerful housekeeper had been with the Drew family for years, ever since Nancy's mother had died when Nancy was very young. Hannah shook her head at the skimpy outfits that Nancy and George were wearing. "Party or no party, I'm afraid you two will catch your death of cold," she fretted.

Nancy pulled a heavy coat out of the closet as George slipped into hers. "Don't worry, Hannah," Nancy said, "we'll be warm as toast in these."

After waving goodbye to Hannah, Nancy and George stepped outside and decided to take Nancy's car, a blue Mustang. Fifteen minutes later Nancy turned the car onto a downtown street. "I think the Razor's Edge is somewhere around here," Nancy said, peering through the windshield. "I don't know why we haven't tried it out before now."

3

"I don't think it's been open too long," George commented. "Dance clubs seem to open and close quickly."

By this time in the evening, most of the shops and businesses were closed, their windows dark and still. As Nancy guided the car around another corner, she and George could see lights and people spilling onto the street in front of them. "That must be it," Nancy said, nosing the Mustang into a space beside the curb. "I didn't realize there'd be such a big crowd—Bess was certainly right about this place being popular!"

Wedged between two taller buildings, the Razor's Edge had a sleek facade of granite and glass. A crowd of teens all wearing summer clothes underneath jackets were lined up in front of a tall, burly doorman who was blocking the entrance. The doorman sported a curly black beard and seemed to be in his early thirties.

"Why isn't he letting people in?" George asked. "Isn't it time for the dance party to start?"

"Bess said the doors would open at eight forty-five, and not a moment sooner," Nancy explained. "I think the managers like to build up anticipation in the crowd before anyone goes inside."

Nancy and George joined the line. "I can't wait to get in," Nancy overheard a young lady

4

saying excitedly to a friend. "I'm such a fan of that French DJ they've got. Etienne Girard. He really *jams!*"

By now the crowd had doubled. A stocky, curly haired guy who was holding a camera lost his balance and tripped over one of the velvet ropes that was separating the club-goers from the entrance. He wore glasses and seemed about twenty years old.

"Get back, you!" the doorman snapped, seizing him roughly by the shoulder and shoving. The guy's face reddened, and he quickly straightened up and slid back into line.

George's dark brown eyes flashed with anger. "That was uncalled for, shoving that guy that way," she muttered to Nancy.

"You're right, George," Nancy replied. The doorman was obviously carried away with his job, Nancy decided. She glanced at the curly haired guy to make sure he was okay. He had lowered his head to hide his embarrassment, but he seemed to be unhurt. Just then the double entrance doors were thrown open, and the teens began streaming inside.

Once inside, everyone stood in another line in the front lobby to drop off coats and jackets with a young woman who was wearing a striped bikini and a welcoming smile. Nancy and George then followed the crowd onto the floor, where they were instantly surrounded by dancers.

The air itself seemed to vibrate with the driving music. Nancy looked around. Real palm trees in planters and man-made Styrofoam boulders were scattered about the edges of a large multileveled dance floor. Here and there throughout the room there were metal steps leading to raised dance platforms, where couples could show off their best dance moves.

The beam of a roving spotlight swept across the room. Those who weren't dancing had picked up creamy tropical drinks and were moving to tables that were jammed against the far wall, directly across from the main entrance. A beach scene from some old surfing movie was being projected onto the wall behind the tables. The entire space had the look of a fun day at the beach.

Nancy nodded toward a set of metal stairs that led up to one of the dance platforms. "Let's climb up there and look around," she said. She and George went up the steps. After dodging the sharp elbows of a guy who was dancing with wild abandon, Nancy and George pushed over to the railing and leaned against it to survey the crowd below.

"Send that guy back to dancing school," George muttered under her breath as the wild dancer fell against her during an off-center spin.

Nancy grinned. "He must have been born with two left feet," she replied.

A tall boy, whom Nancy recognized from her high school class, materialized at her side. "Want to dance?" he asked.

Nancy smiled. "Maybe later, okay? Right now I have to find somebody." She eased away and descended the steps with George. "Let's find Bess," she shouted to George so she could be heard above the music. "I haven't spotted her yet."

Maneuvering across the crowded floor toward the far wall, Nancy spotted a glass-enclosed booth that housed a complicated-looking control panel. Inside the booth was a cool guy, about twenty-one years old. He had a shaved head, a single dangling earring, and wore a wild, orchid-colored shirt. Weaving and bopping to the music, he was holding one end of a set of headphones to his ear while he pressed some blinking lights on the panel.

That must be Etienne, the DJ the girl had mentioned in line, Nancy thought. He was certainly doing a great job that evening. The floor

was crammed with dancers swaying and writh-
ing to the music, which was a driving mix of
technopop and snippets of old sixties songs. The
effect was a compelling mixture of sound unlike
anything that Nancy had heard before. She felt
her feet itching to dance, and she began to regret
turning down the guy who had asked her earlier.

George tapped Nancy's arm to get her attention. "There's Bess, over there by that door," she
said, pointing toward a side exit to their left.
"And *look* what she's wearing!"

Nancy turned her head to focus on where
George was pointing. "Wow!" she exclaimed.

Bess was sitting high atop one of the larger
Styrofoam boulders. She was dressed in a glittering silver mermaid outfit over a flesh-colored
body stocking. Tiny seashells and flowers were
artfully woven into her long blond hair, which
was plaited in a single braid.

Nancy and George threaded their way across
the crowded dance floor to speak with Bess.

"Hi, you guys!" Bess enthusiastically waved a
tail fin at Nancy and George as they approached.
"Isn't the music awesome?"

"Bess, you look absolutely incredible," Nancy
said, smiling. "That outfit is terrific."

There was a soft, popping sound to Nancy's

right. Bess's welcoming smile froze into a startled expression as a camera flash illuminated her face for a moment.

"Thanks for the picture, Bess," a male voice broke in. Nancy turned and recognized the curly haired guy who had tripped over the velvet rope while standing in line earlier that evening. "I'm just taking some shots for my photo album," he explained with a shy smile.

"Sure thing," Bess replied, blinking slightly from the flash. He gazed at Bess for a second, then disappeared into the crowd.

"You know that guy?" Nancy asked curiously.

Bess shrugged. "His name's Tom something. Tom Kragen, I think. He's just a goofy guy from my riding club who's asked me out a couple of times. I've tried to discourage him without hurting his feelings."

"Another candidate for your fan club, Bess?" George asked with a sly grin.

"Him? Ugh! No way!" Bess sputtered.

A tall, olive-skinned man wearing a red silk shirt and gray tinted glasses approached the girls. He appeared to be in his late twenties. "How's your first night going, Bess?" he asked in greeting.

"Just great," Bess replied. She turned to her

friends. "Nancy, George—this is Lonnie Cavello. He owns the *E*—that's what the in crowd calls the Edge."

Lonnie shook hands with Nancy and George. "Bess is our star of the evening," Lonnie said in a friendly fashion. "Because what's a beach party without a mermaid?" He glanced at his watch. "I guess I'd better check with our doorman, Lucas, to find out how big this crowd is getting. We don't want any trouble with the fire marshal tonight." He waved and headed for the front lobby.

"Fire marshal?" Nancy asked. "What's that all about?"

"Lonnie told me there's a maximum number of people the club can hold, or else the fire department can come in and shut the club down," Bess explained. "The city is pretty strict about its fire regulations."

The guy who had asked Nancy to dance earlier that evening reappeared with a friend, and soon Nancy and George were hitting the dance floor, relaxing, and having a good time.

The DJ had just begun a new music set when Nancy caught a whiff of something that smelled medicinal and vaguely sweet. She briefly wondered where the odor might be coming from.

Just then the music died abruptly, and the

dance floor was plunged into darkness. Several dancers let out excited cries.

Then Nancy heard another, more alarming sound—the sound of a dull thud, followed by a frightened scream for help. Nancy's stomach contracted with fear—the cry for help sounded as if it was coming from Bess!

Chapter

Two

BESS! ARE YOU OKAY?" Nancy called into the darkness. She strained to hear a reply, but it was no use. The dancers surrounding Nancy were making too much noise as they chattered and milled about in confusion.

Just then the floor lights came back on. Etienne Girard leaned down to speak into a microphone that was attached to the side of the DJ's sound booth.

"That little interruption was just to keep you on your toes." Etienne spoke smoothly in a charming French accent. "This next song will get them tapping on the dance floor." His words

12

were followed by a crashing wave of sound that introduced the next set.

Nancy craned her neck to catch a glimpse of Bess. She felt a surge of anxiety. Bess was gone!

"Look, George!" Nancy cried, pointing toward the now-deserted rock. "Bess is gone—and I'm sure I heard her yell for help just as the lights went out." Her eyes darted around the room, searching in vain for her friend.

George followed Nancy's anxious gaze. "I thought I heard a scream, too, but I figured it was just someone reacting to the lights going off."

Nancy glanced around, her gaze lingering on the exit door near the rock where Bess had been sitting. "I'm going to look for her," she said. "George, why don't you go inform Lonnie Cavello that Bess is missing. Maybe he knows something we don't."

"Good idea," George said, heading for the front lobby. "I'll check out the rest of the club, too."

Nancy studied the door next to the spot where Bess had been sitting. A cold draft of air was seeping in around the edges of the door. It wasn't fully closed. The edge of the door was separated from the frame by a good quarter inch. Above the metal handle on the door a sign read: Alarm

Door—Do Not Open. Nancy hesitated. Then she took a deep breath and pushed on the door.

It gave way easily. She breathed a sigh of relief when no alarm went off. She stepped through the door and found herself standing in a narrow alley lined with trash cans. There was no sign of Bess.

Nancy scanned the area for any clue to her friend's disappearance. A stiff breeze blew a piece of paper flat against her ankle. As she reached down to brush it away, Nancy spotted a small white object glistening in the light from a single bulb beside the door. She picked it up— and her heart skipped a beat. The object was a tiny white shell attached to a hairpin, just like the ones Bess had been wearing in her hair that evening.

"Nancy!" George said, opening the door and stepping out into the alley. She was followed by Lonnie Cavello. The club owner had removed his glasses, and Nancy could see the concern etched across his dark features. "We looked all over the club, but found no sign of her," George continued. "Did you find anything?"

"I'm afraid so," Nancy said. She held out the shell on the hairpin for them to see. "This is one of the hairpins that Bess was wearing tonight. This proves that Bess went out this way—or was forced to."

"I can't understand this." Lonnie took the shell and turned it over in his hand. "Maybe she felt sick or something and decided to go home."

"No way! That's not like Bess." George shook her head vigorously. "She'd never duck out without an explanation. Besides," George continued, "how far could she get in that mermaid costume she was wearing?"

"And I know I heard her scream for help just as the lights went out," Nancy said. "There's no way she'd just wander off because she wanted to go home." She paused, thinking. "Was that alarm door working earlier today, Lonnie?"

"Yes, I know it was because we just had a fire inspection," Lonnie said. "Why?"

"Because, obviously, it wasn't working just now—or when Bess came out this way," Nancy declared. "We would have heard the alarm."

Lonnie took in a deep breath. "You're right. I didn't think of that. Let's have a look."

Lonnie examined the insulated wiring that ran along the inside of the doorjamb. "It's been cut," he announced in surprise.

Nancy's heart sank. "Which means Bess was probably taken against her will by someone who disabled the alarm system first." She forced her voice to remain steady.

George's face was white with fear. "I'm scared

for her, Nan. What can we do?" Her voice was barely more than a whisper.

"We're going to have to move very quickly, George," Nancy said. "We have to call the police, and then Bess's mom and dad." She dreaded making the call to Bess's parents to tell them what had happened.

"You can use the phone in my office," Lonnie offered.

The three of them went back into the club and headed for Lonnie's office. As they skirted the dance floor, Nancy was oblivious to the dancers and the pulsating music. A scary word was beginning to echo in the back of her mind—that word was *abduction*. Who would want to kidnap Bess, though? she asked herself. And why?

"My office is over there," Lonnie said, gesturing with his hand. They had reached the lobby of the Edge. On one side of it, Nancy could see a wall of frosted glass that separated it from Lonnie's office.

"Do you know why the lights went out just before Bess disappeared, Lonnie?" Nancy asked, following him over to his office door. "There's got to be a connection between the two events. No one could have grabbed her like that if the lights had been on."

Lonnie shrugged. "We've been having problems with the power system ever since Etienne came to work here," he explained. "He's a fabulous DJ, but I'm afraid his sound system has put quite a strain on this old building's wiring."

"Old building?" Nancy remarked curiously as the three of them entered Lonnie's office. "From the outside, the Razor's Edge looks brand-new."

"The former owners gave the old girl a pricey face-lift a few years back to keep up with the times," Lonnie replied. "But actually, this building is over sixty years old, and we're beginning to have more than our share of problems with the wiring and plumbing systems." He sighed, and then he gave Nancy a curious glance. "You ask so many questions, you sound like a detective."

"She *is* a detective," George interjected. "A good one." Although she was only eighteen, Nancy had solved many mysteries in her short career. Now she was praying that her sleuthing skills would help her solve the mystery of her good friend's disappearance.

"I had no idea you were a private eye," Lonnie said. "I'm sure you'll figure out what happened to Bess."

Nancy picked up the phone that was on Lonnie's walnut desk and put in a call to the River Heights Police Department. She spoke to the desk sergeant, briefly describing what had happened, including Bess's scream, the shell hairpin, and the severed alarm wire. Then she pressed down the receiver. "They're sending a patrol car over right away," she told Lonnie and George. "Now for the hard part." She punched in another number.

"Calling my aunt and uncle?" George asked. Nancy nodded her head silently.

Mr. Marvin answered the phone. He took the news of Bess's disappearance calmly, although Nancy could hear his voice thicken with concern. "It sounds like you've done everything that can be done so far, Nancy," he said. "I'll tell Bess's mother. What do you suggest we do?"

"Just stay by the phone, for now," Nancy said, "in case Bess contacts you. I'll follow up here with the police when they arrive."

"Thank you, Nancy," Mr. Marvin's voice cracked just a bit. "I am grateful for everything you're doing."

"Try not to worry, Mr. Marvin," Nancy said, mustering as much reassurance as she could. "We'll find her."

"I know you will," he replied before saying goodbye.

Nancy's heart felt heavy as she hung up the phone. "I'd like to talk to some of your staff people, including Etienne, the DJ," she said to

Lonnie. "I want to ask him about the blackout, if his sound system caused it. I'd also like to check Bess's coat and other things."

Lonnie thought for a second. "I told her to stow her stuff in the dressing room," he replied. "It's just down the hall. I'll show you the way." He led the two girls out of his office.

Crossing the lobby, Lonnie paused to speak with a waiter. "Go get Etienne," he told the young man. "Tell him we're in the dressing area." Then Lonnie reached for the knob of a door hidden in the paneling. The doorway led into a narrow, tiled hallway that was lined with several more doors. "Here's her dressing room."

The cramped room was just large enough for a makeup table and a small bookcase. The walls were bare except for a latched access window. Nancy could hear a sound like gurgling water coming from the other side of the window.

"Where does that window lead?" Nancy asked.

"Into a utility room," Lonnie replied. "It holds the water tank. Why do you ask?"

Nancy paused before answering. "I've learned to observe everything about the place I'm in," she explained. "Sometimes the smallest detail can turn out to be an important clue."

"I see," Lonnie said, sounding impressed.

Nancy spotted some folded clothes that she

immediately recognized as belonging to Bess. She spread them out on the makeup table.

"There's not too much here," Nancy said, disappointed. "Just some of her clothes and jewelry." As she refolded the jeans Bess must have been wearing earlier that evening, Nancy noticed a piece of crimson paper sticking out of one of the pockets. Nancy smoothed out the paper and read it. "It seems to be a flyer about another dance party," she said, showing the paper to George. "An underground party."

"I've got a friend who goes to underground parties," George said. "They're very spontaneous, and you can only find them if you're invited. They're impossible to get to if you don't know the right people."

Lonnie's face reddened as he scanned the flyer. "Those underground parties are really hurting my business," he fumed.

"How so?" Nancy asked.

"With my club I have to pay a lot of overhead —rent, salaries, taxes, and so on. Underground dance organizers just open wherever they please, put the word out, then sit back and rake in the money," Lonnie explained bitterly. "It's really galling."

Nancy looked at the flyer more closely. It was advertising two underground dances: one for that night at an abandoned amusement park on the outskirts of River Heights, and the other for the next night—in the warehouse district. A girl's name was scrawled in purple ink across the top of the paper—Charity Freeborn. The name was written in Bess's handwriting, Nancy noticed.

"Do you happen to know who this Charity Freeborn is?" Nancy asked.

"Unfortunately, I do." Lonnie's words were clipped. "I had to fire her just last week. She was my theme hostess before I hired Bess, but she was unreliable. She got angry when I insisted that she show up for work on time, so I let her go. She threatened to get back at me when I hired Bess to replace her."

Nancy stuck the flyer into her pocket. "Perhaps Charity planned to get back at the club by staging an incident involving Bess," she said to Lonnie. "In any case, I definitely want to ask her some questions."

"I'd stay away from Charity Freeborn, if I were you," a man with a soft French accent said behind Nancy. "She's trouble!"

Chapter

Three

Nancy turned to face Etienne Girard standing in the doorway next to George. Etienne's shaved head and funky clothes heightened the impact of his handsome, fine-boned features.

Etienne stuck out his hand to shake Nancy's. "I am Etienne Girard, the club's DJ. Why did you send for me, Lonnie?" he said to the club owner.

"That new girl I hired, Bess Marvin, has disappeared. We think she may have been kidnapped," Lonnie told him. "Her friends want to ask you a couple of questions."

"Bess, the mermaid girl? Kidnapped?"

Etienne's eyes widened. "I never actually met her, but I would be glad to help, if I can."

"I'm Nancy Drew, and this is George Fayne," Nancy said, shaking his hand. "What did you mean when you said that Charity Freeborn is 'trouble'?"

Etienne hesitated. "Charity's a little—how do you say in English? Volatile. She comes from a very wealthy family, but you'd never know it to look at her. And what a quick temper! She reminds me a little of a French girl I used to know," he said with a sheepish smile. "She has actually quarreled with customers and ended up in fistfights!"

"She sounds like the sort of person who could be capable of seeking revenge," Nancy observed, remembering how Charity had threatened to get back at Lonnie for firing her. Nancy showed him the flyer. "Bess must have had contact with Charity at some point, because she wrote her name on this flyer. And now we know that Charity resented Bess for being hired to replace her. She even vowed to take revenge against Lonnie and the club. I'd like to track her down and ask her some questions. Do you know where she lives?"

Etienne stared at the flyer. "You will not find

her at home because she had some problems with her parents over the guy she's seeing. I am not sure where she is staying. With friends, I think. But I know she never misses a party. If you like, I can go with you there tonight and introduce you to her."

"And who will fill in for you here at the club tonight, Etienne?" Lonnie Cavello's question sounded like a challenge.

"I have a taped music program running now, and I will give you another one that will last the rest of the evening," Etienne replied. "I want to help Nancy and George find Bess."

Lonnie shrugged. "Okay," he said, rubbing his eyes wearily. "I guess I can handle the music myself."

"Do you know why the lights went out earlier this evening, Etienne?" Nancy asked. "It coincided with Bess's disappearance. Lonnie said the sound system might have strained the building's wiring."

Etienne shrugged. "I do not know why that happened. The lights just went out. I was not doing anything unusual with the system then."

"I'll have an electrician check the wiring tomorrow, Nancy," Lonnie offered.

"That'd be helpful," Nancy replied. "You can

ride with me and George if you like, Etienne," Nancy said, taking the flyer back from the DJ.

Etienne shook his head. "I have to go over a few details with Lonnie. I'll meet you at the front entrance of the amusement park in an hour."

Nancy nodded and turned to leave. "That'll give us time to talk to that guy, Tom Kragen," she said quietly to George.

"Tom Kragen? You mean that pesky guy with the camera?" George asked.

Nancy nodded. "He was taking pictures of Bess shortly before she disappeared. Maybe something will turn up on one of the photos that will give us a clue."

Nancy and George went back down the hall-way. Then they headed for the dance floor and climbed a set of stairs onto one of the elevated dance platforms. From there, Nancy surveyed the room. "I don't see Tom anywhere," Nancy said, disappointed. "I'll look up his home tele-phone number after we talk to Charity Free-born."

Nancy's attention was suddenly drawn to a strikingly dressed couple dancing near the exit where Bess disappeared. "I think I saw them dancing near Bess earlier tonight. Let's ask if they saw anything," Nancy said, descending the platform steps.

Nancy and George made their way across the floor to the couple, who were dressed in matching black-and-neon-orange bodysuits. "Pardon me," Nancy said as she tapped the girl's shoulder. "We're looking for a friend of ours, Bess, who disappeared earlier tonight."

"The one wearing the mermaid outfit," George explained. "We wondered if you saw anything."

The girl brushed back her brown bangs. "The mermaid? I was wondering where she went. Is anything wrong?"

"We think she was abducted when the lights went out," Nancy replied.

The girl's eyes widened. "How awful!" she exclaimed.

"We didn't notice anything unusual, really," her partner interjected. "Just that some of the people freaked when the lights blew."

"Did you notice who was in the area around Bess at the time? Anyone who seemed out of place?" Nancy asked.

"Not really," the girl said, shaking her head. "Just some of the people who work here."

"Which ones?" Nancy pressed.

"A couple of waiters, and maybe a doorman or someone like that. Sorry we can't be of more help."

Nancy thanked the couple and wove a path

through the dancers, followed by George. As soon as they reached the lobby, they could see the flashing blue light of a River Heights patrol car strobing through the front windows of the Razor's Edge.

Nancy and George went outside to speak to the officer, a tall, black-haired man whose nameplate read T. Jones. When Nancy introduced herself, the officer gave her a swift, appraising glance. "Say, aren't you the girl who solved that problem they were having over at WRVH-TV last year?" he asked. He was referring to a case in which Nancy had protected the local TV news anchor from a murder threat. Nancy nodded. "That was a good piece of work," the officer said with admiration.

"Thanks," Nancy replied. As she described the events surrounding Bess's disappearance to the officer, Lonnie Cavello and the doorman came up and stood next to them. Nancy noticed that it was a different guy, not the one with the curly black beard. The bearded guy must be on his break, she thought.

After asking a few questions, the officer snapped his notepad shut. "I'll send for someone to dust the door for prints," he announced. "And we'll search the alley again and also check the power, but you probably found the only real piece of evidence, the shell hairpin. Let us know if you turn up anything else."

"I will," Nancy promised. She decided not to mention Charity Freeborn for now, at least until she turned up something specific.

After giving Lonnie her phone number, Nancy and George climbed into Nancy's Mustang to head for the amusement park where they hoped to find Charity Freeborn.

George was still pale. "I'm so worried about Bess, Nan," she said. "I just can't believe something like this is happening."

"I know, George." Nancy reached over and gave her friend a comforting pat. "We'll find her, and the person who's responsible." Her eyes narrowed with concentration. "Let's go over what's happened so far," she said. "It seems odd that Bess was abducted on the first night of her new job, and in a way that was sure to create an incident. That could suggest someone seeking revenge."

"Someone like Charity Freeborn," George suggested.

Nancy nodded. "But it may also be the club that is the intended victim, and taking Bess is just a way to embarrass the club. The kidnapper had to be someone who had enough access to the club to cut the alarm wire on the door and rig the lights to go out. So we're also talking about someone with electrical expertise."

"Which may or may not describe Charity," George echoed.

"We'll learn more about that when we meet her." In the moonlight Nancy could just make out the arcs of the roller coaster tracks rising above them.

"Remember this park, George?" Nancy said, turning into the parking lot. "My dad used to bring us here on weekends. It's too bad it had to close."

The memory made George smile despite her concern for her cousin. "I remember how we had to drag Bess onto the roller coaster. She preferred the house of mirrors."

"Bess does love mirrors." Nancy grinned. Then her expression turned serious again. "We'll find her, George. We've got to."

Nancy and George parked the car and followed a line of teens heading for the darkened front gate.

"The park's closed, how do we get in?" George wondered out loud.

"It looks like everyone's hopping the fence over there," Nancy replied, pointing toward some teens who were scrambling up and over the chain-link fence.

"It feels like trespassing going in when the park's closed down," George commented.

"It is," Nancy replied. "I wouldn't do it, but Bess's life may be at stake. From what I've heard, these underground parties never take place at the same location twice."

As they came up to the point in the fence where boxes had been stacked as steps, Nancy spotted an old clunker of a car approaching. Etienne hopped out and jogged up to them.

Despite the chill evening air, Etienne was wearing his wild orchid shirt without a jacket. Nancy was afraid he was going to get cold, but decided not to say anything.

Nancy, George, and Etienne climbed the boxes to hop the fence and jumped down into the park.

"Tonight's dance is under the old roller coaster," Etienne explained. "And that is where we should find Charity."

Despite the kids moving toward the dance, the park still felt deserted and somehow abandoned. Missing from the scene were the lights and motion of whirling rides, the insistent invitations from sideshow barkers, and the tinny sound of canned music played too loud. Nancy shivered slightly and drew the collar of her coat more tightly around her neck. From the distance she could feel the thumping rhythm of a strong and driving bass line.

The area around the base of the old wooden roller coaster was jammed with kids. They were wearing all kinds of weird, funky clothes—lots of black spandex and hair dyed fuschia and magenta. Spike heels were in, Nancy saw. Someone had brought a handful of California-style outdoor heat lamps to warm up the chill October night. Between the heat lamps and the wild motion of dancing bodies, the scene was very hot indeed.

Music pulsed out from a strange-looking band on a raised makeshift stage. The band members were dressed in yellow and red—even their faces and hands were painted yellow and red. The band's driving technopop sound was amplified to a crescendo by a row of huge speakers that lined the stage.

Some of the daredevils had staked out choice spots to dance high above the crowd on the roller coaster's scaffolding and tracks. They clung precariously to the old frame.

Nancy scanned the area. "Do you see Charity?" she asked Etienne.

The DJ searched the crowd with his eyes. "Not yet," he said. They moved slowly through the crowd, getting jostled from all sides. "Wait a minute! There she is," he said, pointing to a couple dancing near the band.

Nancy took in Charity's appearance. She was about eighteen years old, dressed all in black, her hair sticking out in stiff black spikes. She wore heavy eye makeup, and a row of eight earrings studded her left ear. Overall, Charity had the look of a tough street urchin. Etienne was right, Nancy thought. It was hard to believe she came from wealth.

Charity's eyes widened as soon as she noticed Etienne. "Etienne! *Cheri!*" She threw her arms around the DJ. Underneath the makeup, a soft vulnerability showed on Charity's face.

Charity's dancing partner was eyeing the newcomers suspiciously. He was a muscular, dark-skinned man in his early twenties. "What are you doing here, Etienne?" he asked the DJ abruptly. The man spoke with a lilting accent that Nancy could not place.

"Nancy, George, this is Charity Freeborn and her friend, Gaetan Orakuma," Etienne said, ignoring Gaetan's unfriendly tone. "A friend of theirs disappeared from the club tonight, and we are trying to find her."

"Her name's Bess Marvin," Nancy explained.

"Bess has disappeared?" Charity's eyes widened with concern. "She said she might come to the dance later tonight."

"When did you speak with Bess, Charity?" Nancy asked quickly. "We're trying to find out as much as we can to help the police with their investigation."

At the mention of the word *police,* Charity and Gaetan stiffened visibly. "Charity doesn't know anything about your friend," Gaetan said quickly, stepping between Nancy and Charity.

"That's right," Charity agreed, taking Gaetan's hand. "And right now we have to be going."

Nancy grew suspicious. Why would the mere mention of the word *police* cause them to have such a reaction? "I'm just trying to find out—" she began, but Gaetan and Charity had already melted into the crowd. "Wait a minute!" Nancy called, heading after them.

Nancy crashed into a woman as she pushed her way through the dancers to catch up to Charity and Gaetan.

"Hey!" the woman yelled angrily.

"Oops, excuse me," Nancy muttered. She kept going and finally spotted the couple. They were moving away from the dance area toward a dark section of the park. Nancy followed until she saw them duck behind the carousel. I'm not going to let them get away that easily, she thought to herself.

Nancy doubled her speed and decided to cut across the merry-go-round to intercept them.

The round wooden floor of the carousel groaned slightly as Nancy stepped up onto it. The pastel-colored wooden horses glowed softly under the light from the full moon.

After peering back over her shoulder, Nancy realized she'd lost George and Etienne in the crowd. In fact, this part of the park was completely deserted and, except for the distant hum of music, silent.

Without warning, two figures popped up from behind one of the horses. Charity and Gaetan. Charity, alone, advanced on Nancy menacingly.

"Leave us alone," she growled, reaching deliberately for something under her jacket.

Nancy stiffened as she spotted a flash of metal in Charity's clenched hand. It was a knife!

Chapter

Four

NANCY STARED at Charity. In her peripheral vision she could see that Gaetan had frozen. She held her breath for a moment, wondering what Charity would do.

"Charity, don't," Gaetan spoke softly. At the sound of his warning, Charity blinked, uncertain what to do.

Nancy seized her chance. Her foot flew out in a lightning-swift kick, knocking the knife out of Charity's hand. The knife skittered onto the concrete pavement beside the carousel and spun to a halt about five feet away.

Charity stared at Nancy. "I wasn't going to

hurt you," she said sullenly. "I was just trying to scare you so you'd leave us alone."

Nancy hopped off the carousel, picked up the knife, and hurled it far away. "You shouldn't be playing with knives, Charity," she said furiously. "Lonnie told me you threatened to get revenge for being fired, and your behavior just now makes me believe you're capable of it. If you know anything about Bess's abduction, you'd better tell me."

Charity's eyes grew round with surprise. "You think *I* kidnapped your friend Bess? That's a laugh!" she scoffed. "I bumped into her earlier tonight when I sneaked into the club to pick up some of the things I'd left when I quit. We talked, and I even told her about this party. She said she was going to try to come after she finished working."

"You say you *quit* that job? I thought Lonnie fired you," Nancy said.

Charity shook her head. "He wouldn't give me a raise, so I walked. He told you I threatened him?" she asked. When Nancy nodded, her scowl deepened. "I hope that jerk falls off a cliff," she fumed.

Nancy sighed. Charity was saying Lonnie lied to her about the reason for Charity's leaving the club. The girl's stormy temperament did make her an unreliable source of information, though, Nancy reasoned.

"Was Gaetan with you when you saw Bess?" Nancy asked. Charity paused, then shook her head. "No, Gaetan was practicing with his band all evening," she said. "He was never at the club."

Gaetan stepped forward and took Charity's hand. "Let's leave, Charity," he whispered.

Charity looked at Nancy. "We're out of here," she said, edging away. The couple vanished into the night. This time Nancy let them go. It would be useless to press Charity for more information, she thought.

At that moment Etienne and George arrived at Nancy's side. "There you are, Nancy! We lost you back there in the crowds." George sounded slightly out of breath. "We ran all over looking for you. Did you catch up with Charity and Gaetan?"

"Yes," Nancy said. "Charity explained that she hadn't been fired and that she'd met Bess earlier tonight. I felt as if she and Gaetan were hiding something, though." She then described how Charity had pulled a knife on her.

"I told you Charity has a quick temper."

Etienne shook his head ruefully. "She may have acted that way because Gaetan is hiding from the police."

"The police?" Nancy echoed. "Why?"

Gaetan was from the African country of Angola, Etienne told her. "His visa expired months ago, and he's been avoiding the immigration authorities ever since."

"That's probably why he looked so nervous when I mentioned the police," Nancy remarked as they climbed back over the fence to leave the park. The DJ's rusted old car was still parked close by. "How did you meet Gaetan?" she continued. "Through Charity?"

Etienne shook his head. "Gaetan and I have known each other for years. I met him in Paris, which is my hometown," he explained. "We came to America with big dreams of opening our own music club together. But our dream fell apart pretty quickly." Nancy thought she detected an edge of bitterness in the DJ's voice.

"It sounds like there's bad blood between you two," she commented.

"You could say that," Etienne said. "Gaetan's had it in for me ever since our business plans fell apart. He blames me for the fact that he lost his investment."

"Gaetan and Charity seem like an unlikely couple," George commented.

Etienne nodded. "Their toughest challenge so far has been Charity's parents. They're violently opposed to her romance with Gaetan. I guess because he is from a different background." He shrugged. "I heard that's why she ran away and is living with friends."

"Do you have Gaetan's address?" Nancy asked the DJ as he climbed into his car. "I may need to contact him or Charity."

Etienne scrawled an address on a scrap of paper he pulled from the glove compartment. All of a sudden the DJ seemed in a hurry. "Where are you going now?" he asked Nancy distractedly. Nancy wondered what was prompting his sudden sense of urgency.

"Back to the Edge," Nancy replied. She glanced at her watch. It was past one in the morning. "It'll be closed by now, but I want to take one more look around. It might help me sort through the pieces regarding Bess's disappearance."

Etienne nodded. "Call me at the club tomorrow and let me know what is happening," he said. He threw the car into gear and peeled away, the rear wheels kicking up a spurt of gravel.

"I wonder where he's rushing off to?" Nancy mused as she and George returned to her Mustang.

"Yeah, I didn't know an old car like his could go so fast," George commented dryly.

Nancy realized she was exhausted, but she was determined to continue the search for Bess. "You must be tired, George," she said as she turned the car onto the highway back to River Heights. "Do you want me to drop you off?"

"No way!" George shook her head so vigorously her short, dark curls whipped around her face. "We're in this together until we find Bess."

"I knew that's what you'd say," Nancy replied. She gave her friend an affectionate smile.

On the way back to the Edge, Nancy pulled into the parking lot of an all-night convenience store. She used the outdoor pay phone to call the Marvins.

Bess's father answered the phone. He sounded tense and depressed as he reported they hadn't had any news about their daughter.

Nancy was lost in thought as she returned to the car.

"From the look on your face, Nan, I can tell my aunt and uncle haven't heard anything yet," George said.

Nancy shook her head in reply. "There's something we're missing here, George. Someone went to a great deal of trouble to abduct Bess and must have had a strong motive for doing it." She turned on the ignition. "I know I'm overlooking something important."

"I can't imagine why *anyone* would have it in for Bess," George said with a catch in her voice. "She doesn't have an enemy in the world."

"The only person we've turned up with a possible motive for abducting her is Charity Freeborn, but she denied being fired and threatening Lonnie. However, she did behave in a guilty way when I confronted her tonight. First she took off, and then when I cornered her she pulled a knife on me."

"On the other hand, if she did take Bess, why would she be out dancing all night?" George countered. "It doesn't make sense."

"You're right, George." Nancy sighed out loud. "It's way too early to call her a solid suspect."

The roads were almost empty because of the late hour, so Nancy and George made it back to the front entrance of the Edge quickly. Nancy parked at the curb and turned off the lights. She sat silently, leaning on the steering wheel, sorting out her thoughts. "Tomorrow I'll call information for Tom Kragen's number and try to get those pictures of the party. Then I want to track down Charity again and follow her," she said. "Maybe she'll lead us somewhere."

The engine of a car coughed to life somewhere nearby. Nancy sat up, alert. "That sounds like it's coming from the alley behind the club," she said, cocking her head. She reached for the car door and opened it. "I'm going to see what's going on back there."

"I'm right behind you," George replied. She had to sprint to keep up with Nancy, who was racing down the sidewalk toward the corner of the alley.

The girls could hear car tires screeching down the alley. Nancy reached the opening and peered down it. She found herself caught in the glare of a pair of high beams. The lights belonged to a car that was wildly backing down the alley, away from Nancy and George. There was a scraping sound followed by a crash as the vehicle knocked over a metal trash can before it disappeared around the far corner of the alley.

Nancy grimaced. "I couldn't even make out what color that car was," she said to George. "Could you?"

George shook her head. "Those headlights were too blinding," she replied.

Nancy and George jogged down the alley toward the club's rear door. Nancy stopped short suddenly and put out a restraining hand to George. "Wait a second, George. Do you hear that noise?"

George looked confused. "What noise?" she asked. Then she cocked her head to listen for a moment. "It sounds a little like a kitten mewing," she said slowly.

Nancy nodded and started poking around the trash bins, which were surrounded by heaps of industrial-size garbage bags. She stepped back, startled, when there was some movement at her feet, and she caught sight of a tumble of hair and sequins. Then her heart flipped with joy as she saw a groggy but familiar face staring up at her.

"George," Nancy whispered, kneeling down. "Look—*it's Bess!*"

Chapter

Five

B ESS!" GEORGE'S FACE reflected her relief, then her fear as she took in Bess's pallor. "Is—is she okay?" she asked Nancy.

Bess was wearing a denim jacket draped over the shoulders of her mermaid's costume. Underneath the jacket, Nancy could see that her hands were bound. Nancy loosened the ropes, then held Bess by the shoulders and gently raised her to a sitting position. She could see Bess's eyes slowly begin to focus.

"Can you speak, Bess?" Nancy felt so anxious for her friend that she could barely utter the words.

"Yes. I think so." Bess's voice was weak, barely

audible. "Nancy—George. Thank goodness you're here," she said, trying to smile.

"Are you hurt, Bess?" Nancy asked quickly. "Maybe we should call a doctor."

"No, really, I'm okay. Help me up." Bess swayed slightly as Nancy and George helped her to her feet. "I must have been knocked out for a while." Bess smoothed the tattered remains of her mermaid's costume and looked around at the smelly garbage alley. "Yuck! I feel like yesterday's dinner special."

George giggled with relief. "You *must* be okay if you're making jokes," she said, giving her cousin a warm hug.

Nancy took the denim jacket off Bess's shoulders. "This is a man's jacket," she observed. "It probably belongs to your abductor." She examined the lining. "It's pretty small, and it has a French label."

"French? Like Etienne?" George gasped.

"I guess anyone could wear a French label, but I *did* notice that Etienne wasn't wearing a jacket tonight." Nancy spoke slowly. She looked down at Bess and noticed a narrow band of cloth around her neck. "That looks like a blindfold."

Bess nodded and started to speak, but Nancy stopped her. "You can tell us everything in a little while," she said, putting a protective arm around her friend's shoulder. "First, we're going to call the police and your mom and dad, then take you home and get you something hot to drink."

"Tell us exactly what happened, Bess—from the moment the lights went out at the Edge." Nancy spoke as Bess took her second sip from a mug of hot tomato soup that Mrs. Marvin had prepared.

Nancy, Bess, George, and the Marvins were sitting around the table in the Marvins' kitchen. Nancy and George had brought Bess directly home from the Edge, where she had a joyful reunion with her frantic parents. The police decided to hold off interviewing her until the next day.

Bess leaned back and closed her eyes. "That guy who took my picture, Tom Kragen, came by to ask me for a date. He was being kind of a pest. After a while he finally took the hint and wandered off. Then the lights went out, and someone grabbed me by the shoulders." Bess shuddered slightly. "I yelled out for help, but someone clamped some kind of wet cloth over my nose and mouth—it made me real dizzy. That's when I blacked out."

"A wet cloth," Nancy said thoughtfully. "It was probably soaked with something that would knock you out." Nancy paused for a moment. Then she cocked her head. "Did the cloth smell kind of sweet? Like syrup?"

Bess nodded. "Come to think of it, it *did* smell sweet—sickeningly sweet," she recalled.

"What do you think was on the cloth, Nancy?" Mr. Marvin asked. He leaned forward to hear her answer.

"I'd have to examine it to be sure, but I'll bet it was soaked in ether." Nancy recounted for them how she had smelled something sweet and medicinal just before the lights went out at the Edge earlier that evening. "I remember reading somewhere that ether has a sweet odor, and it would have been able to knock out Bess the way she described. Doctors used to anesthetize people for surgical procedures with ether," she explained.

"Whatever it was, I don't remember anything until I half woke up on a cold, gritty floor. I couldn't see anything because they had blindfolded me."

"You say 'they' blindfolded you. What makes you think it was more than one person?" Nancy asked.

"I was in and out of consciousness the whole time, but I distinctly remember hearing two men arguing. It sounded like they were on the other side of a wall." Bess paused, taking another sip of the steaming soup. "It was real muffled, but I think one of them wanted to let me go."

"Were you able to recognize either man's voice?" George asked.

Bess shook her head. "The sound was too muffled. And I'm afraid I wasn't thinking too clearly at the time."

"What happened next?" Nancy prompted her.

"I wasn't aware of anything else for a while. Then someone came in and lifted me up. The blindfold slipped for a second, and I caught a glimpse of a green eagle tattoo. I think it was on an upper arm."

"That means he was wearing a short-sleeved shirt," Nancy said quickly. "Kind of an unusual way to dress on a cold October night."

"Yes, but everyone from the beach party at the Razor's Edge was wearing short sleeves," George volunteered.

Nancy nodded. "You're right, George," she agreed. "It could easily have been someone from there. What happened next?"

"I was loaded into a car that had a rough-sounding motor. Then after a distance I was dumped out, I guess in that alley behind the club," Bess explained. "That's when you and George found me, Nancy."

"So, you were first taken away from the club

and then brought back to it," Nancy said slowly. "It's almost as if someone knew that George and I were heading there and would find you."

"But no one knew we were going back to the club after leaving the amusement park," George pointed out.

"The only person we told was Etienne," Nancy said slowly. "And you mentioned that the car had a rough-sounding motor, Bess, like—"

"Like that old clunker Etienne was driving," George chimed in excitedly. "Oh, Nancy, do you think he could have been involved? But he was at the club all night after Bess disappeared."

"He could have had an accomplice. But I can't think of an apparent motive. You said you never even met him, Bess."

"The DJ? No, I know who he is, but I didn't meet him. I was too busy." Bess rubbed her eyes wearily. "I'm really beat," she announced with a yawn.

Mrs. Marvin looked worried. "You need your sleep now, Bess. I'll turn your bed down." As she passed by the chair where Nancy was sitting, Bess's mom leaned down to whisper to her. "Bess's father and I would appreciate it if you and George would spend the night, Nancy. It's getting awfully late, and I think Bess would welcome the company."

"Of course," Nancy replied quickly. George nodded her head. Nancy was glad to be staying over. It would be a good idea to keep an eye on Bess for the time being. Bess had agreed to stay home for the next few days in the company of at least one other person. She had mentioned that her abductors may have argued about letting her go. Nancy thought there was a chance they might change their minds and come after her again.

It was three A.M. After calling home to let their parents know they'd be spending the night at Bess's, Nancy and George got ready for bed.

"You guys can borrow my nightgowns," Bess offered, holding out a delicate gown to George.

"Peach lace and silk." George grinned, holding up the gown between two fingers. "Just my style."

"You'll have to rough it for one night, George," Bess said, teasing her tall, athletic cousin. "I'm afraid I'm fresh out of flannel sleep shirts."

Nancy was distracted. "You look like you're figuring something out, Nancy," George observed. "What is it?"

Nancy shook her head. "I was just thinking about that green eagle tattoo. It sounds pretty unusual. And about that guy Tom Kragen. You said he was being kind of a pest, Bess. What kind of pest?"

"The won't-take-no-for-an-answer kind of

pest," Bess replied. "I tried being tactful when he asked me for dates in the past, but tonight I had to let him know there wasn't a chance."

"How did he take it?" Nancy asked.

Bess shrugged. "He was a little annoyed, and kind of slunk off." She frowned, fastening the buttons on her mauve dressing gown.

"What are you thinking, Nancy?" George asked as she slipped into a goose down sleeping bag that Mrs. Marvin had retrieved from the attic. "Do you think this Tom Kragen could have been involved in Bess's abduction?"

Nancy shook her head. "Not from what we've heard so far. But he *was* taking pictures shortly before she was grabbed. I want those pictures to see if they reveal anything unusual."

Bess crawled under the covers. "I think I once heard Tom say he works part-time at his father's granite quarry," she said, her voice muffled by her pillow.

"Good," Nancy replied. "We'll look for him first thing tomorrow morning."

Soon, Nancy could tell from the sound of their even breathing that Bess and George were sound asleep. She turned over restlessly in her sleeping bag and stared at the clock radio on Bess's side table. The glowing green numerals read three-thirty A.M.

Nancy was unable to drift off to sleep. Lying half-awake, she listened to the breeze rustling in the trees outside Bess's first-story window.

Suddenly another noise—a sharp, scraping sound—startled Nancy completely awake.

Nancy slipped out of her sleeping bag and crept toward Bess's window. The window curtains were backlit by the light from a full moon. Nancy's pulse quickened as she watched an inky black shadow move across the windowpane. It was the shadow of someone prowling around outside.

Chapter

Six

WITHOUT MAKING A SOUND, Nancy grabbed the Princess phone from Bess's bedside table and dialed 911. "Break-in in progress at the Marvin residence," she whispered, and gave the police dispatcher the address.

The shadow moved away from Bess's window. Nancy dropped the phone and darted to the window to catch a glimpse of the intruder. She got a brief impression of a man in a jacket running across the yard.

"What is it, Nancy?" George's sleepy voice rose up from her sleeping bag. Then she sat up alertly. "Did something happen?"

Bess was wide-awake by now. "I heard it, too,

Nancy. I'm scared that it's going to happen all over again," she moaned.

"Someone was trying to break into Bess's room," Nancy said tightly. "I've already called the police." Even as she spoke, Nancy could see the pulsing blue light of a police patrol car flash across the lawn.

"There are your prowler's footprints," the officer said, pointing to an impression in the soft soil beneath Bess's window.

The police had responded to Nancy's call for help within minutes. Nancy, Bess, George, and Bess's parents were clustered around the tall, rangy River Heights police officer, discussing the attempted break-in.

"This has gone too far. I want round-the-clock protection for my daughter until we get to the bottom of this," Bess's father said to Officer T. Jones, who had responded to the first report about Bess's abduction.

Flashlight in hand, Jones knelt down to study the footprints. Nancy looked over his shoulder at the prints. They were large—about a size thirteen, Nancy estimated—and the sole had the distinctive waffle-pattern of an expensive leather running shoe.

"Did you get a look at the man?" Jones asked

Nancy. Nancy described what she'd seen. "I'm betting this attempted break-in is connected to Bess's abduction," she told him.

"I'm sure you're right," Jones replied. "I'm going to call my lieutenant to get them to assign someone to watch your house, Mr. and Mrs. Marvin." He turned away and lifted a bulky two-way radio from his leather belt. After exchanging a few words with someone back at the police station, he nodded to Nancy and the others. "They'll be posting someone to watch the house for the next couple of days. I'll stay until they get here."

"That's great," Nancy said. After talking with the officer for a few more minutes and learning that the police had turned up no leads from their investigation of the Razor's Edge, she and George turned to follow the Marvins back into the house. Nancy mulled the recent events over in her mind. Bess had been released, but now there'd been this prowler incident. Was Bess still in danger? And again, Nancy asked herself, Why Bess?

As soon as they were back in the house, Nancy, Bess, and George fell into exhausted sleep.

By the time Nancy opened her eyes the next day, it was late morning. After saying goodbye to

Bess and her parents, Nancy and George stopped off at their homes to change clothes and grab a bite of breakfast. Then they drove directly to the Kragen quarry.

Although it was Saturday, the quarry was in full operation. The quarry site was an open granite pit set in the midst of some rolling hills about ten miles east of River Heights.

As they turned into the parking lot, Nancy and George were startled by the rumbling of an underground blast, which was followed by ground tremors.

"This must be what an earthquake feels like," Nancy said, stopping the car. The girls could see a mushroom cloud of dust and debris rising from the huge granite pit.

"It would take a lot of dynamite to blast through all that solid rock," George said, taking in her surroundings.

Nancy nodded. "These guys must really know how to deal with explosives," she commented.

Nancy and George got out of the car and headed toward a trailer that was being used as an office. It was set about twenty yards back from the edge of the quarry. A sign on the trailer said: KRAGEN QUARRY—DANGER—EXPLOSIVES— VISITORS MUST BE ESCORTED.

"Hey, you there!" An older man came running across the parking lot toward Nancy and George. He had a big stomach and curly hair that was beginning to turn gray underneath his yellow hard hat. He was an older version of Tom Kragen. "You looking for somebody?" he asked.

"Are you Mr. Kragen?" Nancy inquired. When the man nodded, she added, "We're looking for your son, Tom."

Mr. Kragen became unexpectedly pleased. "Well, now," he said with a smile. "You must be Bess Marvin. Tom's told me a lot about you."

"No, I'm not Bess," Nancy said, taken aback. "I'm Nancy Drew, a friend of hers. But I need to talk to Tom about Bess."

"Oh." Mr. Kragen's face fell slightly. "Sorry about the mix-up. Tom told me he was dating a beautiful blond lassie named Bess, and you certainly fit the bill. You'll find Tom in the office over yonder," he said, waving his hand toward the trailer. "Grab a couple of hard hats if you're going to be here more than a few minutes," he added.

"Why do you think Tom Kragen lied to his father about being involved with Bess?" George whispered as they climbed two stairs up to the office door. "That's really weird."

"I don't know," Nancy replied. "But he definitely has some explaining to do."

Tom Kragen was sitting behind a desk, surrounded by piles of paperwork. In a business setting, he looked much older than he had at the club the night before.

"Hello there. Can I help you?" Tom pushed his glasses farther up on his nose as he greeted them. The thick glasses magnified his pale green eyes, making them appear larger than normal. He was wearing a light blue shirt and running shoes. "I remember you," he said slowly. "You two were with Bess at the Razor's Edge last night. Have a seat."

"That's right," Nancy said, taking a chair. "I'm Nancy Drew, and this is George Fayne."

"Is Bess here, too?" Nancy detected a note of anxiety in Tom's voice. She shook her head.

"Bess is the person I came here to talk about." She told him how Bess had been abducted the night before. Tom acted shocked.

"Who do you think did it?" he asked, adjusting his glasses again.

"That's what we're trying to find out," Nancy said. "You were taking pictures at the club last night, weren't you?"

"Yes." Tom nodded. "In fact, I know I have a

few shots of Bess. She looked so great in that mermaid outfit."

"Did you notice anything unusual, or see anyone who looked out of place?" Nancy asked.

Tom shook his head. "I was too busy taking pictures to notice, I'm afraid."

"Have the pictures been developed yet? I'd like to see them. The ones with Bess in them, plus any others you have of the party," Nancy said.

Tom rose from his chair. "I've got a makeshift darkroom in the back."

Nancy and George followed Tom down a narrow hallway into a small room that had been converted into a darkroom. "One advantage of being the boss's son—you get to pursue your hobbies on company time," Tom said with a grin.

In the glowing red light of the darkroom, Nancy peered at several photographs that Tom had tacked onto a corkboard wall. A couple of the photos featured Bess wearing her mermaid outfit at the club the night before.

Nancy glanced at some of the other photographs that were scattered about the room. "Here's a photograph of Bess at her riding club," she observed.

Nancy suddenly became aware that many of the pictures on the walls were photos of Bess that had been taken at various times over the past year. It almost looked as if Tom had been doing a photographic study of Bess. She thought it seemed strange. "You seem to have taken quite a few pictures of Bess," Nancy said to Tom in a neutral tone.

Tom suddenly became aware of what Nancy was thinking. "I think Bess is really photogenic," he said hastily. "I'm starting a portfolio that I hope will land me a photography job one of these days."

Nancy decided to press Tom about his father's earlier comment. "George and I met your father just outside the trailer. He said you'd told him that you and Bess were dating," Nancy said. "Why did you say that?"

The dim light of the darkroom couldn't hide the embarrassed blush that had crept up Tom's neck and face. He turned away to fumble with some beakers on the worktable. "I guess he just misunderstood when I said that Bess and I are friends," he said awkwardly. Tom quickly untacked the pictures of the party from the corkboard and offered them to Nancy. "Here, you can take these if you want."

"Thanks," Nancy said. She decided to wait until they were outside to study the photographs more closely. "By the way," she added, keeping her tone casual. "You left the party kind of early last night. Didn't you like the music?"

"Oh, I'm not much of a dancer." Tom opened the door of the darkroom. "I came back here to develop the photos." He led the way back to the main office. "Since you're here, why don't I give you a tour of the quarry," he added.

Nancy hesitated, then nodded her head. "Sure, why not," she agreed. The tour would give her a chance to talk to Tom on his own turf.

As they left the trailer, Tom handed Nancy and George a couple of yellow hard hats. "We have to be really careful around here, what with all the blasting we do," he explained. Remembering the prowler's footprints from the night before, Nancy studied Tom's shoes. They looked fairly large —they could be a size thirteen, Nancy thought. She purposely hung back a few steps for a moment while they walked through the loose earth toward the quarry. She noticed that his footprints didn't have the same distinctive waffle-pattern that had been under Bess's window.

It was almost noon, and the quarry seemed almost deserted. "Everyone on lunch break?" George asked.

Tom nodded. "Since everyone's gone, we can go right up to the edge of the pit," he said, leading Nancy and George through the gate of a safety chain-link fence. They walked about fifteen yards to the rock-strewn lip of the vast, yawning gravel pit.

The mouth of the pit was surrounded on two sides by rocky outcroppings from the surrounding hills. Far below, Nancy could see some ladders and equipment that workers had left behind. From that vantage point, the equipment looked like children's toys.

Nancy, Tom, and George walked along a downward sloping, narrow ledge that ran underneath a sheer wall of rock at the edge of the pit. Looking at the rock walls, Nancy could see long, grooved striations in the rock. "That's where we drill down to put in the dynamite," Tom explained. He suddenly turned his head, listening. "I think I hear my dad calling. Just a second." He turned and retraced his steps along the ledge until he was out of sight.

"Where'd he go?" George asked after a moment.

Nancy shrugged. "Let's not wait for him," she said. "I can always talk to him later. Right now I want to get back to the car and study these photographs."

"Good idea," George said, turning to leave. "I think I've seen as much of a quarry as I care to see in one lifetime."

A sharp, cracking sound came from somewhere overhead. Nancy and George stopped and looked up at the rocky outcropping. To her dismay, Nancy saw that part of the face of the wall had dislodged and was sliding down into the gravel pit. A large boulder was jarred loose by the falling earth and began tumbling down the wall. Tumbling straight toward Nancy and George!

Chapter

Seven

"LOOK OUT, GEORGE!" Nancy cried out. The boulder was almost upon them. She sprang forward and pushed George ahead of her on the ledge. Jagged pebbles bit into Nancy's palm as she and George fell into a sprawling heap on the gravel.

The boulder landed with a sickening thud just inches behind Nancy's heels. A cloud of dust and fine debris rose from the site.

George was the first to clamber to her feet. "Are you okay, Nan?" she asked anxiously. "It looks like you're hurt."

"I'm okay." Nancy picked herself up from the dusty ground and gingerly tested her limbs. She felt a little tenderness on her palm and knees where the gravel had scraped them when she fell.

The loud, long wail of an emergency alarm siren shattered the air. A handful of quarry workers, some holding half-eaten sandwiches, came running toward the pit. They were led by Tom Kragen's father. "What happened? Are you girls hurt?" Mr. Kragen's voice was tight with concern.

"We're okay, but it was a close call," said Nancy, whose pulse was still racing. "That boulder down there almost flattened us."

"Where's Tom?" Anger crept into Mr. Kragen's tone. "This area's not safe. Did he let you out here without an escort?"

"I'm right here." Tom appeared behind the group of men who had accompanied Mr. Kragen. "I was out here with them. Then I thought I heard you calling me."

"You *never* leave visitors alone here! *Never!*" Mr. Kragen's voice roared with rage. "These young ladies could have been killed."

Tom lowered his eyes and poked at the dust with his shoe. "I'm sorry," he said, not quite meeting Nancy's eyes.

"What would cause a rockslide like that?" Nancy pressed the elder Kragen.

"We constantly use explosives, which makes

for a very unstable ground environment," Mr. Kragen explained. "The boulders you see all around us could let loose any second."

As if to underscore Mr. Kragen's words, the earth under their feet trembled slightly. "Let's get out of here," he added quickly.

Tom remained silent as they walked back to the office. Nancy and George refused Mr. Kragen's offer of a cup of hot tea and said goodbye.

"Wow, that was too close." George shook her head as they climbed back into Nancy's car. "Tom's father was really giving him a hard time for leaving us there alone, wasn't he?"

"Yes, but Tom didn't seem too upset about it," Nancy commented.

"I can see wheels turning behind those blue eyes, Nan," George said shrewdly. "What are you thinking about all this?"

Nancy turned the key in the ignition, and the Mustang's powerful engine roared to life. "Maybe it's nothing, but I find it interesting that Tom led us into a dangerous area and then left, just moments after I confronted him about his relationship with Bess."

"You mean the fact that he lied to his father about dating her?" George asked.

Nancy nodded. "That, plus the fact that he has

taken all those photographs of her over the past year. Some of the shots looked as if they were taken without her being aware of them. It's possible that he's obsessed with her."

"He wouldn't be the first guy," George said, grinning.

Nancy frowned as she maneuvered her car onto the highway. "I'm serious, George. People with real obsessions have been known to do desperate things, things like . . ."

"Like kidnapping?" George said, finishing Nancy's thought with a somber question.

"Exactly." Nancy nodded. "I also couldn't help noticing that he had rather large feet, just like the prowler at Bess's house last night. And he doesn't have an alibi for what he did after the party at the Edge. He *said* he came back here to develop the pictures, but he'd have been alone. I think I should do some more checking." She steered the car out of the parking lot. "If he was behind it, he must have had an accomplice." She frowned. "And he must have had access to the club to rig Bess's abduction."

"That's right," George remarked. "He would have had to have been able to cut the lights and the alarm door wire, and have gotten hold of the ether to knock her out."

Nancy nodded. "He has quite a collection of

chemicals in his darkroom, I noticed. I'm sure he'd have no trouble getting access to something like ether."

Nancy pulled up to a roadside stand that was selling pumpkins for Halloween. "I can't believe it's almost Halloween," George said. "Why are we stopping here?"

Nancy slowed the car. "Now that we're out of the Kragens' sight, I want to look at those pictures."

Reaching into her purse, Nancy pulled out the stack of photographs she'd gotten from Tom Kragen. She set aside the three of Bess sitting on the rock in her mermaid outfit. The rest of the shots focused on the beach decor and people dancing. "I don't see anyone I recognize," Nancy said, thumbing through them. "Wait a second," she said, retrieving a photo. "Look at this."

George peered at it. "I see Etienne in the background in his DJ's booth. Who's he talking to? They look like they could be arguing."

Nancy bent her head over the photograph to study it. "That's Gaetan Orakuma, Charity Freeborn's boyfriend," she said, surprised.

"Did Charity mention that Gaetan was at the party last night?" George asked, scrutinizing the photo.

Nancy shook her head. "She specifically said that Gaetan was *not* at the party—and that she herself had left well before the club opened."

"I guess this proves that's not true," George said, tapping the photo. "I wonder why she lied?"

"Yes, and I wonder what Gaetan and Etienne were arguing about?" Nancy said. "I couldn't help noticing that there was tension between them at the amusement park last night."

"Didn't Etienne say they'd planned to open a club together when they came to America?" George asked.

"Yes, and he said that Gaetan blamed him for their plans falling apart, and his losing his investment. Losing money can ruin a relationship very quickly." Nancy shrugged. "But I don't see a connection with Bess's abduction." Nancy paused, considering. She was lost in thought for a long moment.

"I know that look, Nan," George said to her friend. "What are you thinking about?"

"Just something that strikes me as odd," Nancy replied. "Remember how eager Etienne was to come with us to look for Charity last night? He left Lonnie in a lurch for someone he'd never even met."

"You think Etienne was tagging along just to

keep an eye on what we were doing?" George asked. Nancy nodded. "But why?" George continued in a bewildered tone.

"Why, indeed? And why did Charity lie about Gaetan's being at the club last night? I'm also remembering the fact that Etienne has a car with a rough-sounding motor, just like the one Bess said brought her back to the club last night. And depending on where Bess was being kept, Etienne could have had time to retrieve her and take her to the club after he left us at the park."

Nancy dropped the photos into her bag. "Let's go find Etienne. It'll give us a chance to question him about his relationship with Gaetan, and maybe check out his car." Nancy rose from the table. "After that, I want to pay a visit to Gaetan. I'm beginning to become suspicious of this Etienne-Gaetan-Charity triangle. There's more to it than anyone's told us so far."

Nancy drove to the Razor's Edge to look for Etienne. On the way to the club, they picked up hamburgers and shakes at a fast-food place and ate in the car.

As soon as they arrived at the Razor's Edge, they found Lonnie Cavello busy at work directing the setting up of elaborate Halloween decorations.

"Hi, Nancy. Hi, George," he said, greeting

them. The club owner was arranging a life-size skeleton inside a fake coffin. "Bess called this morning and caught me up on everything that happened since I saw you last night. I must say, it's all pretty hard to believe. She said she didn't feel like coming in to work today, and I can't blame her."

"We're just happy she's back safe and sound," Nancy said. "I'm still trying to figure out why she was abducted."

"I know, it's—*Lucas!* I said pile the pumpkins by the *back* wall, not the side," Lonnie said, snapping at the tall, bearded doorman whom Nancy had seen guarding the club entrance the night before.

"Whatever you say, Lonnie." The doorman's thick arm muscles bulged as he lifted several large pumpkins and carried them to the back wall.

Lonnie sighed. "I always have to tell Lucas everything twice. He's a good bouncer because he intimidates everyone with his size, but he's not too swift up here," Lonnie said, tapping his head.

"It looks like you've almost got everything ready for Halloween," Nancy said, wanting to guide him back to the subject of Bess's abduction.

Lonnie nodded. "Tonight's just the preview,

but tomorrow we're throwing a huge Halloween bash. It'll be a costume party, of course, and we're pulling out all the stops. There'll even be a five-hundred-dollar-prize for best costume. You girls should come."

"We will," Nancy promised. "Right now we're looking for Etienne. Is he around?"

"Why do you need to talk to him?" Lonnie turned away to fuss with an arrangement of colored autumn leaves.

"I'm still trying to get to the bottom of what happened to Bess last night," Nancy replied. "I'm wondering if you can tell me anything about Etienne's relationship with a guy named Gaetan? There's apparently some bad blood between them."

"Gaetan Orakuma?" Lonnie made a gesture of distaste. "Isn't he Charity's boyfriend? I hear he's as crazy as she is."

"She may be crazy, but last night she denied that you fired her, Lonnie. She said she quit."

Lonnie looked agitated. "What would you expect her to say? That I gave her the boot? No way she'd admit that." Lonnie spat out the words. "You could probably tell she flies off the handle pretty quick. I couldn't have someone like that working here."

"I guess you're right," Nancy said. She had to

admit that Charity had a temper like Mount Vesuvius.

Lonnie turned away impatiently. "You're on a wild-goose chase, Nancy. I suggest you leave this investigation to the police, who know what they're doing. You're likely to stumble into something you can't handle."

Nancy was surprised by Lonnie's outburst. "I can take care of myself," she said evenly. "If you could just tell me where I can find Etienne?"

Lonnie shrugged. "Etienne doesn't report for work until about seven P.M., but maybe you can find him at home." Lonnie pulled a pen from his shirt pocket and scribbled the DJ's home address on the back of one of the club's business cards. "I'll write down my name and number, too, in case you need to get in touch with me," he said.

"Thanks," Nancy said, taking the card. She and George got back into her car and headed to Etienne's house, which was an apartment in a small, run-down complex. "Number six," Nancy said, peering out from her car at the number on the front door. "This is where Lonnie said he lives."

Nancy parked the car, then she and George walked up to the front door. Nancy raised her hand and knocked. To her surprise, it swung open under her light rap. "Etienne?" Nancy called out uncertainly. There was no reply. Nancy called out again, then she took a couple of steps into the small living room. "Etienne?" Nancy repeated.

"Oh, no!" Nancy heard George say from somewhere behind her. George was pointing into the brightly lit kitchen. Nancy looked, and then her hand flew up to cover her mouth. A man's body was sprawled faceup across the kitchen floor, with purple marks around his throat. It was Etienne, the Razor's Edge DJ—and he seemed to be dead!

Chapter

Eight

FEELING HER STOMACH TURN, Nancy nevertheless took several swift steps toward the kitchen. She knelt down and felt for any signs of life.

"I'm afraid he's dead, George," she said, her voice catching in her throat. She raised her head, listening for any sound that might indicate that the intruder might still be lurking around.

Hearing nothing, Nancy started thinking ahead. "We're going to have to put in a call to the police right away," she said. Nancy used Etienne's wall phone to call the River Heights police. When the desk sergeant answered, she asked for Detective B. D. Hawkins, a homicide detective with whom Nancy had worked on another case involving murder.

After speaking to B.D. for a few minutes, Nancy hung up and turned back to George. "They're coming over right away," she said. "But before they get here, I want to take a look around. We'll have to be careful not to disturb any possible evidence."

Nancy conducted a quick visual search of Etienne's apartment for any clue that would help her identify his murderer. She turned up nothing. All at once Nancy paused and sniffed the air. "Do you smell that, George?" she asked her friend.

George took in a deep breath. "No, I don't— wait a minute. You mean that sweet smell, like pastry dough?"

Nancy nodded. "That's the same smell I caught at the club last night. I'm sure it's ether."

"Ether," George said. "Isn't that the stuff you figure Bess's kidnapper used to knock her unconscious last night?"

"Yes, and now it seems as if ether was used to knock Etienne out before strangling him," Nancy replied.

"That means that whoever abducted Bess last night could have murdered Etienne," George said somberly.

Nancy nodded. "There's no question we're probably dealing with an extremely dangerous person, George." She was excited by the discovery of the connection between the two crimes, yet puzzled. What on earth could the connection be? Nancy knew she didn't have much time to figure out the tie-in between the two crimes. But it seemed almost certain that Bess's kidnapper was also Etienne's killer and would stop at nothing— not even murder.

George shivered. "Bess is very lucky to be alive," she said in a shaky voice. "When I think that she could have been in the hands of a psycho last night, whoever he is . . ." Her voice trailed off.

"Or *she*," Nancy reminded her, thinking of Charity Freeborn. "In fact, a woman might be even more likely to use a knockout potion like ether than a man, to compensate for lack of physical strength."

A River Heights Police Department patrol car pulled up outside. As B. D. Hawkins, the tall, lanky detective, climbed out of the front seat, Nancy and George went out to greet him. Behind the wheel was T. Jones, the officer who had responded to Nancy's call at Bess's home the night before.

"Hi, Nancy! What've you got here?" As usual, B.D. got right down to business.

"Murder by strangulation, it looks like. The victim is Etienne Girard, who worked at the Razor's Edge dance club. He's in the kitchen," Nancy said, leading the way back into the apartment.

B.D. followed Nancy into the kitchen, where he knelt and briefly examined Etienne's body. "You're right. He was strangled," the detective stated. "The coroner'll be along in a little while." He stood up and stared down at Nancy. "I know you well enough to know that you've probably already taken a look around," he said with a ghost of a smile. "What have you turned up?"

"I caught a whiff of something that smelled like ether," Nancy answered. She filled B.D. in about Bess's kidnapping the night before, and the probable use of ether in that incident.

"Then whoever kidnapped your friend could have murdered this guy, as well," B.D. said thoughtfully. "Is there motive?"

Thoughts of Tom Kragen, Gaetan, and Charity raced through Nancy's mind. "I have suspicions, but no solid evidence," she told the detective. She handed him the photo she'd picked up at Tom Kragen's, the one that showed Gaetan and Etienne fighting. She briefly described who Gaetan was. "Gaetan's girlfriend said he was never at the Razor's Edge last night. But this photo clearly shows he was there, and that he was probably having a nasty argument with Etienne."

B.D. peered at the photo. "Hang on to that photo, Nancy. I may need it later as evidence," he said. "We now have to treat everything we turn up as part of an official murder investigation."

Just then the wall phone in Etienne's kitchen rang. Motioning for the others to remain quiet, B.D. answered the phone. He listened for a moment and then hung up. "It was just someone soliciting business," he said.

"That phone call gives me an idea," Nancy said. "I wonder if Etienne has an answering machine. Maybe he has some old messages that will give us a clue about what happened, or what he was up to."

George nodded. "There is one. In his bedroom," she said.

Nancy, George, and the two officers went into Etienne's sparsely furnished bedroom. A slim black answering machine sat on Etienne's desk.

B.D. pressed the Play button. They heard the metallic gibberish of the message tape rewinding.

Then a heavily accented voice, distorted with rage, came over the speaker.

"Etienne, you better pay me the money you owe me, or I'm coming after you! I'm going to kill you!" The message ended abruptly as the caller slammed down the phone.

Chapter

Nine

"DO YOU HAVE ANY IDEA who that was?" B.D. asked Nancy. "He could very well be our murderer."

"I know exactly who it was," Nancy said slowly. The caller's lilting accent was easily recognized by her. "The man who threatened to kill Etienne is Gaetan Orakuma."

"Gaetan Orakuma?" B.D. repeated the name. "Tell me more about him."

"He's a former friend of Etienne. My understanding is that they had some business plans that fell through," Nancy explained.

"He must have thought that Etienne owed him

money," the detective said. "People have been murdered over that kind of thing before."

Nancy explained to the detective how Charity and Gaetan had lied to her about being at the Razor's Edge. "Gaetan's girlfriend, Charity Free-born, even tried to attack me with a knife when I questioned her about Bess's disappearance. They certainly acted like they were hiding something. And there's no question that that was Gaetan's voice on Etienne's answering machine, threatening to kill him."

"Then Gaetan could be our link between the two crimes, the kidnapping and Etienne's murder," B.D. replied.

"That would be pretty stupid of Gaetan to leave a message threatening Etienne just before killing him," George pointed out.

Nancy paused, thinking. "You're right, George. That would seem to indicate that the murder wasn't premeditated. He would never have made that threat if he were intending to follow through on it because he'd be booked in an instant. So he must have killed Etienne in the heat of anger. But then," she continued after a brief pause, "the use of ether to knock him out indicates otherwise. It indicates premeditation."

"We'll figure out all the missing pieces as we go along." B.D. shrugged. "At the moment this

Gaetan Orakuma is our most likely suspect in the murder, and probably in the kidnapping, as well. I'll have to bring him in for questioning. Do you happen to know where he lives?"

Nancy nodded. She dug into her purse where she had shoved the slip of paper Etienne had given her the day before with Gaetan's address on it. She handed it to B.D.

The coroner had arrived and was in the kitchen. "Hey, B.D., did you see the tattoo," the coroner called into the living room.

In the kitchen the coroner, a small man dressed in a dark suit, was examining Etienne's right arm. "Look at that," the coroner said, pointing to a tattoo on Etienne's arm. "Isn't that a piece of work? Haven't seen one of those rising phoenix tattoos since I was in Europe with the army."

Peering over B.D.'s shoulder at the tattoo, Nancy gasped. It looked like an ornate green eagle tattoo, just as Bess had described seeing on the arm of one of her abductors! The coroner asked them all to leave before he slipped the body into a body bag.

In the living room Nancy told B.D. about the tattoo that Bess had seen the night before. "Bess said she saw a green eagle tattoo on the arm of the kidnapper who let her go." This meant that

Etienne was probably the half of the kidnapping team who had released Bess, Nancy realized. Her thoughts were racing. Could Etienne and Gaetan, and perhaps even Charity, have been involved in an abduction scheme that went awry? But why? Perhaps, she reasoned, they'd been planning to demand a ransom for Bess, but then Etienne had had second thoughts? And what about Tom Kragen? Nancy hadn't forgotten about the pale, young man—he seemed to be the only person so far who had a clear motive for the kidnapping itself. Was there any connection between him and Etienne, or Gaetan?

"If Etienne was one of Bess's kidnappers, that certainly puts a whole new twist on this thing," B.D. said. "We'll try to sort it out back at the station once we haul in Orakuma for questioning."

B.D. held the door open for the coroners' men as they wheeled the gurney outside. "The homicide squad will go over this place with a fine-tooth comb," he said to Nancy after the ambulance pulled out. "In the meantime I'm going to round up Gaetan."

"I have a couple more things I want to check out," Nancy said.

B.D. nodded and headed for his cruiser. "Call

me at the station with anything you dig up," he said. "I'm always happy to have my assistant sleuth on the job," he added with a grin. Then he hopped into his cruiser and Jones pulled away.

Nancy sat in her car, the keys balled up in her hand. "Well, it looks like B.D. is hot on the trail of Etienne's murderer," George said to her, breaking through Nancy's thoughts. "I can't believe Gaetan killed him—although there *did* seem to be bad blood between the two."

"I'm not completely convinced that it was Gaetan who killed him," Nancy said, starting the engine and pulling into traffic. "There's no question that Etienne was up to his eyeballs in some kind of nasty business. We're practically positive he was one of Bess's kidnappers, but his murder could be totally unrelated to his quarrel with Gaetan."

The sun hung low on the western horizon. "It's dinner time," Nancy said. "Let's go back to Bess's house. I want to see how she's doing, and it'll give me a chance to tell her what happened to Etienne, and also what we found out about Tom Kragen today."

A patrol car was sitting in Bess's driveway when Nancy and George pulled up. "I'm glad to see they're keeping her under surveillance," Nancy said. "Now that it seems like Bess's kidnapper may be a murderer as well, she could be in more danger than ever."

Bess's mother was setting out fried chicken, peas, and mashed potatoes as they went inside. Mr. Marvin was working late at the office, she told the girls.

"I'm trying to get Bess to eat," Mrs. Marvin said. "You two are just in time to join us."

"That makes my mouth water just looking at it," George said hungrily, eyeing the dinner her aunt had spread before them.

Bess greeted them all with quick hugs before joining them at the table.

"Would you two please tell my mom that a kidnapping is *no* excuse for going off a diet?" she said with a laugh. Then she sighed and reached for a chicken leg. "Well, maybe just this once," she muttered, taking a bite.

Nancy filled her in on the day's events. Bess's blue eyes widened when she heard about Etienne's death. "Even though I didn't meet him, it's awful to hear that he was killed. And you say he was one of the people who abducted me?"

Nancy described the tattoo she'd seen on Etienne's arm. "It was a green phoenix, rising out of the flames," she said.

Bess nodded vigorously. "That's it exactly. It

just looked like some kind of eagle to me," she said.

"Then there's no question that Etienne was one of your kidnappers, Bess," Nancy said. "And the other one, the one who probably killed Etienne, is a cold-blooded murderer. The question is, who was his accomplice? And *why* did they abduct you?"

Bess shook her head, bewildered. "I just can't imagine how all this happened, or who's behind it," she said.

Nancy went on to describe what had happened earlier in the day at the Kragen quarry, including all the photographs that Tom had taken of Bess over the past year, and the fact that he claimed to be dating her.

"Tom Kragen and *me?* Yuck!" Bess said indignantly. "I'm really going to give him a piece of my mind the next time I see him."

"The important question is, could he have been involved in your kidnapping? He's certainly obsessed with you. After we confronted him about lying about his relationship with you, he led us out to a hazardous area and took off, leaving us alone."

"Yeah, we nearly became mashed potatoes under a boulder," George said, taking a huge bite of food.

THE NANCY DREW FILES

"Is there any connection you know of between Tom Kragen and Etienne?" Nancy pressed.

"Like I said, I'd never even *met* Etienne, so I can't imagine a connection at all," Bess said helplessly. "So Etienne was the one who dropped me off in that alley," she continued thoughtfully. "I wonder why?"

"He may have realized his accomplice was extremely dangerous, and so he changed his mind about the abduction," Nancy said slowly. "And he paid for that change of heart—with his life."

"Poor guy," Bess murmured.

"What do you mean, 'poor guy'?" George replied, scoffing. "He abducted you, Bess."

"I can't help feeling sorry for him," Bess said in a whisper.

Nancy's brow was creased with concentration. "Bess, I'm wondering what else you can recall about what happened last night before you were abducted. Any little thing at all might help. How about earlier in the evening, when you first got to the club?"

"I arrived at the club, and one of the waiters let me in. Then I wandered around, looking for the dressing room. I went down the hallway and walked into the wrong room. I stumbled into some kind of utility room. Lonnie was in there

88

Chapter

Ten

INSTANTLY REALIZED she had triggered
arm when she opened the office doo[r]
company was probably being sum[moned]
hat very moment. Her heart thumpe[d]
Nancy figured that she probably ha[d]
minutes to get away.

her teeth because her mission ha[d]
cy wheeled around and sped back
ence. George was waiting.

hat happened?" George asked as she
e fence for Nancy. "Did you get

not," Nancy replied breathlessly,
rom under the fence. "We'd better

fixing a water tank and talking to that huge doorman. Lucas I think his name is. They acted kind of startled, and I was embarrassed to be wandering around, so I backed out fast. When I finally found the dressing room I discovered Charity Freeborn rummaging through some drawers in the dressing table. She kind of freaked out when I came in."

"Yeah, she told us she had to sneak in to collect some of her things," George commented.

Bess nodded. "That's what she told me, too. We talked a little bit about some dances around town, then she gave me that flyer. I changed into my mermaid costume and went out on the floor."

"And you stayed there until the club opened?" Nancy asked.

Bess nodded. "That's about all that happened until the kids were let in. Then Tom Kragen kept bugging me for a date. And after that I spoke with you and George."

"Not much to go on," Nancy said. "I still can't see a connection between you and Etienne and Gaetan Orakuma, or how Tom Kragen might fit in with the other two." She paused, thinking. "Did you see a fight between Etienne and a tall, dark guy last night, Bess?" She showed Bess the picture of Etienne arguing with Gaetan.

Bess scrutinized the photo uncertainly. "I

think I saw him somewhere around just before the lights went out, but I can't be sure," she said. "I was too busy fending off Tom Kragen."

George finished the last of her dinner and pushed her plate back. "I'm beyond stuffed," she groaned. "That was delicious, Auntie—as usual."

Nancy rose from the table. "Thanks, Mrs. Marvin. I hate to eat and run, but George and I have to do some more work tonight."

"Where are you going?" Bess asked.

"To find Gaetan and Charity again, but first I want to make a quick stop at the Kragen quarry," Nancy replied. "I want to search the office for anything that would tie Tom to the kidnapping, or to any kind of connection with Etienne."

By now it was dark. The Kragen quarry grounds were dark and forbidding as Nancy and George parked the car on the street nearby. Nancy checked around for any signs of guards or employees, but there was no one in sight. She grabbed a flashlight and her special detective's tool kit from the glove compartment. Then she and George walked up to the fence that surrounded the quarry. The chain-link fence was secured with a huge padlock.

"How're we going to get in?" George whispered.

Nancy surveyed the fence. T[...] that it was wired. "Let's look[...] the fence—someplace big en[...] through," she said. "Otherwise[...] it."

Nancy and George walked[...] ter of the fence, checking for[...] a corner, Nancy saw that[...] separated from one of th[...] spot. She grasped the meta[...] and back, opening a gap a[...] "Let me try first," she s[...] crawling through. Nancy[...] as the jagged edge of the[...] she scrambled up on th[...]

George tried to fol[...] impossible to squeeze[...] through the opening.[...] said, disappearing to[...]

Nancy took her fl[...] the trailer. Seeing[...] out her lock pick a[...] swung open.

Nancy was just[...] she heard a soft[...] moment she fou[...] glare of a secur[...] sound of multi[...]

N[ANCY][...] security a[...] A security[...] moned at t[...] with panic.[...] only a few[...] Gnashing[...] failed, Nan[...] toward the f[...]

"Nancy, w[...] held open t[...] inside?"[...]

"I'm afraid[...] crawling out f[...]

get back to the car pronto, George. I'm sure a security company is sending a car around right now."

The two girls hustled back to the Mustang and pulled away from the curb. When they were less than a quarter mile away from the quarry, they passed a sleek white-and-blue security patrol car. The car's yellow roof lights were flashing as it headed the other way. The officer at the wheel took no notice of Nancy and George.

Nancy breathed a sigh of relief. "Whew, we barely got away that time," she said.

"What were you hoping to find?" George asked.

"Something solid to tie Tom to the kidnapping," Nancy replied. "The photos I saw in his darkroom earlier, and the fact that he lied about dating Bess, may indicate that he's been following her, or worse."

"Do you want to try again after the security patrol leaves?" George asked.

Nancy shook her head. "With that alarm system, it's too risky to go back unless I'm sure of finding something. Let's call B. D. Hawkins and find out what he's turned up so far on Gaetan."

Nancy stopped at a pay phone to call the police detective. B.D. took her call right away.

"Nancy, I'm glad you called," the detective said. "I was just leaving for the night."

"Did you find Gaetan?" Nancy asked.

B.D. sighed. "No, we went to that address you gave me, but he'd already left. It looked as if he left in a hurry, too. There was stuff strewn all over the place."

Just how a guilty party would respond, Nancy thought to herself.

Nancy chatted with the detective a few more minutes, then hung up and turned to George. "Gaetan's running from the police. He abandoned his apartment, and B.D.'s tracking him down. In the meantime let's do a little more digging on our own."

"Where do we start?" George asked.

Nancy thought for a minute. "Let's start with Charity's house, if we can find it. I want to talk with her parents to see if I can get a lead on where she might be staying. And then I remember from Bess's flyer that there's another dance party scheduled for tonight at a loft in the warehouse district. We can go there to see if anyone's seen Charity or Gaetan. It's a long shot, but worth a try."

Nancy lifted the phone book that was attached to the pay phone by a thick metal cord. "Freeborn is an unusual last name," she said, thumbing through the book. "There probably won't be too many of them. Here it is," she said, running her finger down the page. "There are two Freeborns listed."

George peered over her shoulder. "That listing for 'B. Freeborn' says they live at Twelve Regent Court. Isn't that a really fancy part of town?"

Nancy nodded. "And from what Etienne told us, I'll bet that's where they live. Let's head there first."

B. Freeborn's house was an elegant, three-story brick dwelling set back on a wooded lot behind a screen of hemlocks. It looked like a replica of a British manor house. Nancy pulled into the circular drive, where a couple of expensive luxury sedans were parked. A uniformed maid answered the doorbell.

"I'm a friend of Charity's," Nancy said. "Is she home now?"

The dark-haired maid seemed confused and uncertain. "Um—no," she said. "I'll tell Mr. Freeborn that you're here." Nancy felt a surge of excitement as she and George followed the maid into a formal living room. She'd found the right house!

The room was furnished with ornately carved, silk-covered furniture. "This room looks like people never use it," George whispered, taking in the array of expensive porcelain on the highly polished wooden side tables. "I'm almost afraid to breathe in here."

"I know exactly what you mean, George," Nancy replied with a grin.

A man cleared his throat in the doorway just behind Nancy. Turning, she saw a tall, patrician man standing there. "I'm Bradley Freeborn, Charity's father," he stated simply. Mr. Freeborn was wearing a cream-colored cashmere blazer, and had streaks of gray in his dark hair. He had a serious, but not unfriendly, expression on his face. "You know my daughter, Charity?" he asked, reaching out to shake their hands.

Nancy nodded. "I'm Nancy Drew, and this is George Fayne," she said. She decided not to reveal the real reason that she was looking for Charity. "We thought we'd stop by to see if Charity was around. There's a party tonight we wanted to invite her to."

"Well, I wish I could be of some help," Bradley Freeborn said with a sigh. "But I simply don't know where she is." Nancy could see worry lines etched on his brow. "We had a quarrel—a stupid quarrel over her boyfriend, and she took off without a word. Her mother hasn't left her bed in days, she's so worried."

Nancy felt sorry for Charity's father. He was obviously distraught over his daughter's absence. "I saw Charity at a dance last night," Nancy said, trying to reassure him. "She was fine at that time."

"You did?" Mr. Freeborn's eyes lit up. "I'll tell her mother. That'll make her feel much better."

A brass pendulum clock on the mantelpiece over the fireplace chimed eight o'clock. Nancy and George turned to leave. "If I see Charity, I'll tell her that you want her to come home," Nancy said softly.

Nancy thought she saw tears welling in the corners of Mr. Freeborn's eyes. "Thank you, Miss Drew," he said with a grateful smile.

After saying goodbye, Nancy and George headed for the warehouse district.

The warehouse district, which was normally busy with trucks delivering freight and goods during the day, was almost totally deserted at night. Here and there, the girls could see hunched-over figures pushing shopping carts and the campfires of homeless people glowing in the corners of vacant lots.

"We're getting off the beaten track, aren't we?" George observed warily.

Nancy clicked on her high beams to read a

street sign ahead of them. "Here we are, I think. This is where the dance is tonight," she said, turning down the side street.

A row of parked cars stretched along the street in front of them. Nancy pulled into an empty spot, and then she and George followed a group of young people to a nondescript, gray metal door. A guy wearing black baggies and suspenders stood by the door, taking money. "The party's on the sixth floor," he announced.

Nancy and George paid their five dollars each and climbed the six flights of stairs to an upstairs loft. The loft was basically one large, open room with redbrick walls. House music was blasting from a set of oversize speakers that someone had hung from the ceiling.

Nancy recognized some of the same faces she'd seen at the amusement park the night before. Underground parties obviously drew from a crowd of regulars. She hoped that someone would have heard of Gaetan and Charity's whereabouts.

The teens were dressed in their coolest outfits for a special dance competition. The crowd formed a semicircle around the couples who were competing. Nancy and George stood near the back of the crowd, applauding as the male dancer of the couple threw his partner into the air in a spectacular flying twist.

"Those guys are really good," George commented enthusiastically.

"Why don't you grab a guy and get out there, George?" Nancy asked with a chuckle.

George shook her head. "I'm all left feet on the dance floor," she said ruefully.

Getting back to the business at hand, Nancy checked around for anyone she recognized so she could ask about Charity and Gaetan. Then her heart skipped a beat. There was Gaetan, standing talking to the DJ! "George," Nancy muttered under her breath. "Look over there, by the music console."

George followed Nancy's glance. "It's Gaetan!" she gasped. "That's pretty amazing that he'd show up in public tonight, with the police looking for him," she said.

"I'd like you to go find a phone somewhere and call B.D.," Nancy said. "Tell him that Gaetan's here. I'm going to have a talk with him."

"Okay," George replied. "It may take me a while. I didn't see too many pay phones around here while we were driving over."

As soon as George left, Nancy walked toward Gaetan. He spotted her and instantly tried to melt into the crowd. Nancy blocked his retreat by stepping around him.

"Not so fast, Gaetan," Nancy said swiftly. "You have some explaining to do."

A scowl crossed his face. "What are you talking about?" he snapped. "Didn't you bother me and Charity enough yesterday?"

"I came to ask you some questions about Etienne," Nancy replied.

"Why don't you ask him?" Gaetan replied, turning his back on her. It looked as if he was getting ready to leave.

"I can't ask Etienne, because Etienne is dead," Nancy said evenly, waiting for his reaction.

Gaetan froze in his tracks. Then he spun around and stared at Nancy. "What do you mean, *dead?*" he whispered.

"Etienne was murdered—strangled. I was there today when the police found a threatening message from you on his answering machine," Nancy explained.

"So the police must think *I'm* the one who murdered him," Gaetan said weakly. Nancy nodded. He dropped into a sitting position on a folding chair. "So that was why the police were at my apartment tonight. I was in the process of moving, and when I came back to pick up some things, I saw squad cars all over the place." He held his head in his hands. "I thought they'd come to deport me because of my visa problems."

"Why did you threaten to kill Etienne, Gaetan?" Nancy asked him.

Gaetan pulled a white handkerchief from his pants pocket and mopped his brow. "I spouted off while I was angry, but I didn't mean it. I needed the money so that Charity and I could get married," he said.

Nancy wanted to believe what Gaetan was saying—that he hadn't killed Etienne. Maybe he had an alibi, she thought. "Where were you and Charity all day today?"

"I was moving. Charity and I were making trips to my new place in a van I rented," he said. "I don't think we spoke to anyone else all day."

"The police aren't going to buy that alibi, Gaetan," Nancy said. "They may even try to tie you into Bess's abduction. I know for a fact that Charity lied about your not being at the Razor's Edge last night. I have a picture of you and Etienne arguing at the club."

Gaetan grimaced. "I know she lied about that. She just thought you were butting into our private business, so I guess she lied to protect me."

"Protect you from what?" Nancy pressed.

"Charity knows I've been having problems

101

with immigration, and she doesn't want me to be deported back to Angola," Gaetan said. "Etienne and I both put some money into a plan to open a club, and I went to the Edge last night to see if I could get some of it back. We had words, then I left."

Charity appeared at Gaetan's elbow. "Gaetan? What's going on?" she asked, looking from Gaetan to Nancy.

"Etienne is dead," Gaetan said softly. "Murdered." Charity squeezed her eyes shut. Gaetan held out his arms and she went to him, letting herself be enveloped in his embrace. They held each other for a long moment. Nancy could see that they were very much in love.

"How could anyone kill Etienne? Who did it?" Charity's voice was muffled against Gaetan's shoulder.

"Gaetan," Nancy asked. "Do you have any idea who could have murdered Etienne? Did he have any problems or enemies?"

Gaetan shook his head. "I only recall that he had worries about this job. I think the Razor's Edge was having financial problems. But then, Etienne's life was filled with money problems," Gaetan said.

"What kind of problems was the club having?" Nancy asked.

Gaetan shrugged. "I think I remember him saying the club could go out of business if things didn't turn around."

"I believe you, Gaetan, when you say that you didn't kill Etienne," Nancy said. "But the police might see things differently. It would probably be best if you turned yourself in."

Gaetan shook his head desperately. "I can't do that. At the very least they'll deport me, and then I'll never see Charity again."

Nancy glanced over at Charity. "We saw your father tonight, Charity," she said.

"My—my father?" Charity stammered. "How was he?"

"Worried," Nancy said flatly. "He said he wants you to come home."

Charity buried her face in Gaetan's shoulder. "I can never go back without Gaetan," she said.

Nancy decided not to argue with her. She pulled a piece of paper and a pencil from her bag and wrote something on it. "Here's my father's name and office number," she said, handing the paper to Gaetan. "He's a very good lawyer. I think you're going to need one."

"Thanks, Nancy," Gaetan replied.

Suddenly there was a commotion at the front door of the loft. A handful of heavily armed officers, led by Detective B. D. Hawkins, entered the room. Someone cut off the music, and a hush fell over the crowd.

B.D. spotted Nancy and Gaetan right away. It was so quiet that they could hear his leather cowboy boots squeak as he strode across the room.

"You're under arrest, Gaetan," he said softly. "Let's go quietly, shall we?"

Gaetan's shoulders slumped forward. B.D. pulled a pair of handcuffs from his leather belt and snapped them around Gaetan's wrists.

"Gaetan, no!" Charity cried. Nancy watched the tears stream down her face.

Nancy felt conflicted. She had been the one who had tracked down Gaetan and called the police, but now she thought he might be innocent of Etienne's murder. But it was too late—Gaetan was being arrested!

Chapter

Eleven

THANKS, NANCY," B.D. said as the police led Gaetan away. "You really helped us land this suspect."

"Thanks, but I'm beginning to wonder if we got the right guy," Nancy said. "I spoke with Gaetan, and I think he might be innocent."

"We'll figure it out now that we have him in custody," B.D. said. He studied Nancy's stricken expression. "Don't worry. You did the right thing in calling us. He was wanted by the police." B.D. turned to leave. "I forgot to tell you, Nancy. The coroner's report came in—Etienne had traces of ether in his system. So you were right about the kidnapping and the murder being connected."

He left after promising to call her the next day to report the results of Gaetan's interrogation.

George appeared at the front door. "I saw them take Gaetan away," she said. "Charity was following them. So I guess that settles the case, huh?"

The arrival of the police had broken up the party. There were a few people still standing around, but most were hurrying out the door. Nancy turned to leave. "I'm not so sure, George. Gaetan is the obvious suspect, but I can't see him as a murderer—or as a kidnapper."

Nancy's thoughts were racing as she and George returned to the car. If, as she suspected, Gaetan wasn't responsible for the kidnapping or Etienne's murder, she was back to square one.

"I want to check over all the evidence from a fresh perspective," Nancy said. "I think we're dealing with a very clever criminal—someone who's able to cover his tracks very well."

"What do you have in mind?" George asked.

"I want to investigate Tom Kragen again. I can't forget the fact that he has been following Bess around, pestering her for dates and taking pictures. And he has access to chemicals such as ether, which was used in both the kidnapping and the murder."

They drove on for about fifteen minutes. As

they neared the residential section of River Heights, Nancy kept glancing into the rearview mirror. "What are you looking at, Nancy?" George asked curiously.

"That car with the broken headlight has been behind us ever since we left the warehouse," Nancy said. "I'm going to try something. Hold on, George."

Making sure the two-lane highway was clear in both directions, Nancy suddenly twisted the Mustang's steering wheel with a violent motion. The car barely slowed as it performed a nimble U-turn in the middle of the road.

The car that had been behind Nancy and George came to a confused halt as the Mustang spun around and passed it going the other way. Nancy caught a glimpse of the startled driver. She recognized the bearded, hulking man at once.

"That's Lucas, the doorman at the Razor's Edge," Nancy exclaimed. She was extremely surprised. "I think he's been following us!"

Nancy peeled away, leaving the other car far behind.

George peered out the rear window as they pulled away. "I wonder why the doorman would follow us?" she asked in a bewildered tone.

"That's what I'd like to know," Nancy replied,

really puzzled. "I'm trying to figure out what possible connection he could have to Etienne, or Bess's kidnapping."

"Well, he and Etienne worked together," George began.

"Yes, and . . ." Nancy paused, then snapped her fingers. "Now I remember that one of the dancers said she might have seen a doorman around Bess right before the abduction." Nancy's voice was growing increasingly excited. "And Lucas wasn't there when the police first came to investigate the abduction. Remember? There was another doorman on duty. I didn't put the two things together at the time." She glanced at her watch. It was very late. "It's too late to do anything else tonight, but I want to pay him a visit tomorrow, and maybe ask Lonnie a few questions about him, too."

"He's so creepy." George shuddered. "I wouldn't want to tangle with him."

Nancy took a different route back to George's house. They made plans to meet in the morning to continue the investigation.

Walking up the steps to her front door, Nancy realized that she was extremely tired. She and George had been pursuing the investigation practically nonstop since the day before.

As Nancy entered the foyer of her home, she spotted light coming from under the door of her father's study. That meant he must still be up. She tapped lightly on the door.

"Nancy?" She heard her father's deep, reassuring voice. "Come on in."

Nancy stepped into the study. Carson Drew was sitting in a leather wing chair, reading a book. His wavy dark hair was flecked with silver at the temples, and he was wearing his favorite ivory-colored cardigan. Carson set the book aside and smiled at his daughter.

"Were you waiting up for me, Dad?" Nancy greeted her father with an affectionate hug.

Carson shrugged sheepishly. "I wanted to hear how your investigation is going."

Nancy filled her father in on the recent developments, including Etienne's murder. When she described her meeting with Gaetan, Carson's expression grew concerned. "This Gaetan could be a murderer, Nancy," he pointed out. "I hate to see you taking those kinds of risks."

"I think he's innocent, Dad," Nancy insisted. "I gave him your name and number to contact as a lawyer."

Carson sighed. "Of course I'll talk to him, and help in any way I can," he said. "Just promise me you won't take any unnecessary risks from now on."

"Of course." Nancy gave her father a swift kiss on the cheek and said good night. She went upstairs and fell onto her bed without bothering to change into her nightclothes. She quickly fell into a deep, dreamless sleep.

The next day was bright and cold. Traces of frost etched delicate, lacy patterns across the Drews' kitchen windows.

As soon as she was out of bed, Nancy downed a mug of steaming hot chocolate and some granola. She hurried through breakfast, eager to continue her investigation into Bess's abduction and Etienne's murder.

Because the Razor's Edge wouldn't be open at this hour, Nancy decided to visit Tom Kragen. She put in a call to the Kragen quarry and asked for Tom.

"I'm sorry, Tom isn't in," the woman replied.

Nancy thought fast. She had to find out where he was. "Oh, that's too bad, because he wanted me to deliver these papers—he said they were extremely urgent," she lied.

"I don't think he was planning to come in today," the receptionist said, hesitating. "Maybe

you could take them to him at the DoubleTree
riding stable—he's taking his lesson there."

Nancy thanked the woman and hung up. She
felt a surge of excitement. It had been a snap
finding out where he was! Now she'd have a
chance to confront him with a few questions.

She could feel the leaves crunch under her feet
as she walked outside, heading for her car. Nancy
knew where the stables were, and she drove
directly there. Finally pulling into a driveway
along a winding country lane, Nancy spotted
Tom right away. He was doing a cool-down walk
on a spotted bay horse in the center ring. He was
alone.

Nancy parked her car and approached the ring
where Tom was riding. She leaned against the
corral fence and waited to catch Tom's attention.

It didn't take long. Tom's head swiveled
around as he spotted Nancy. He turned the
horse's head and trotted over to where she was
standing.

"You again." Tom's voice was uncharacteristi-
cally curt. "What do you want? Didn't you get
your fill of trouble at the quarry yesterday?"

Nancy became suspicious at his rude tone. "I
just wanted to thank you for giving me those
pictures of the party at the Razor's Edge," she

said. "The police are using one of them in their investigation."

"Yeah, it was a tough break, that DJ getting killed," Tom said.

Nancy locked her gaze on his. "How did you know I was talking about the murder and not Bess's kidnapping? The murder hasn't been publicized yet."

Tom was taken aback. He fumbled with the horse's reins. "I—I heard about it this morning, from a friend," he stammered unconvincingly. Then his scowl returned. "I don't owe you any explanations. Stop following me around, before you have another accident."

"You mean, stop following you like you've been following Bess?" Nancy pressed. Tom jerked his horse's head around and took off across the ring.

Nancy backed away and returned to her car. She'd shaken Tom up, at least. It even sounded as if he'd given her a veiled threat when he talked about her having another "accident." If he was hiding anything about the kidnapping or Etienne's murder, maybe this confrontation would provoke him into tipping his hand.

After stopping to pick up George, Nancy drove directly to Bess's house. She immediately noticed that the police patrol car was missing from the

Marvins' driveway. "I wonder why the police left," Nancy said to George.

Inside the house Bess was busy at work sewing a costume for that night's Halloween party at the Razor's Edge. "Hi, you guys," she greeted them. "How do you like this fifties carhop idea for a Halloween costume? It'll be such a hoot to zoom around on roller skates all night."

"That looks great, Bess," Nancy said distractedly. "What happened to your police protection? Why isn't the officer outside anymore?"

"With that guy, Gaetan, in jail, I guess the police think the crisis is over." Bess snapped off some thread with her teeth. "They still haven't figured out why Etienne was in on the kidnapping, though."

So the police really honed in on Gaetan as a suspect, Nancy realized with a sinking sensation. She'd have to put in a call to her father's office to find out whether Gaetan had contacted him.

"I need to use your phone, Bess," Nancy said.

Carson Drew's secretary put her call through right away. "Gaetan called me from jail about fifteen minutes ago," he told Nancy. "I'm on my way to the station to interview him."

Nancy hung up the phone, feeling that she'd done as much as she could for Gaetan at the moment. She turned around to talk with George and Bess, describing to Bess how the doorman had followed them the night before.

"Lucas followed you home last night?" Bess asked in disbelief.

Nancy nodded. She told Bess how they'd lost him by pulling the daring U-turn. "Do you know Lucas at all?" she asked her friend. "Tell me what he's like."

Bess shrugged. "Lucas is such a weird dude," she said. "He never really talks to anyone but Lonnie. I barely saw him except for that time when I stumbled into the room where they were fixing the water tank. He looked kind of scary." Bess continued working on her costume. "What are you going to wear to the Halloween party tonight, Nan?" she asked.

Nancy considered the possibilities. "I guess I could wear my ninja outfit from a couple of years ago."

"Oh, that was a great costume," Bess said enthusiastically. "I remember you looked really cool in that."

"And with that black mask, no one was able to tell it was you!" George chimed in.

Nancy paused thoughtfully. "I hate to ask you this after all the work you've done, Bess, but would you mind skipping the Halloween party tonight?"

Bess acted shocked. "Why? Do you think I'm still in danger?" she asked.

"I'm not convinced that Gaetan was the person behind your kidnapping or Etienne's murder," Nancy explained. "Until we're positive, I think it would be best for you to remain in hiding."

"No way!" Bess's blond curls bobbed as she shook her head. "I'm going stir crazy, cooped up in this house."

Nancy sighed. "At least play it safe by wearing a costume that conceals your identity. You can trade costumes with me."

Bess looked down at her handiwork. "All right," she said reluctantly. "I was hoping to wow them with my skating moves, though."

"My mom made me a really cool Western costume," George said. "Complete with blue jeans and a lasso."

"A lasso could definitely come in handy if we spot any cute guys," Bess said mischievously.

Nancy glanced at her watch. "Let's head for the club, George," she said. "I want to be there as soon as Lonnie and Lucas arrive."

"I'll go with you," Bess said, starting to rise.

Nancy shook her head no. "Please indulge me by laying low for the rest of the day," she urged.

"Okay, Nan." Bess grinned. "But all of a

sudden I feel like I've got two mother hens watching over me!"

After leaving Bess's house, Nancy and George headed to the Razor's Edge. They found Lonnie Cavello working at the sound booth. He greeted Nancy and George with a somber expression. "The police told me about Etienne's death. Such a tragedy—he was a gifted sound man." He shook his head. "And to think it was a murder. At least they have a suspect in custody. That Gaetan Orakuma and his wild girlfriend are two of a kind."

Nancy decided to get right to the point. "Do you know where your doorman Lucas is? I need to talk with him."

Lonnie's eyebrows shot up in surprise. "Lucas? He's got the day off. Why?"

"He was following me and my friend George last night."

"Maybe it was just a coincidence." Lonnie's brow knitted together in a frown. "Or maybe he was on some misguided mission to help sort out what's happened over the past few days." The club owner threw up his hands. "In any case, I'll have a talk with him."

"Did you have an electrician check the wiring, yet, Lonnie?" Nancy asked him. "We still don't know what caused the power to go out when Bess was abducted."

"I've been so busy, I forgot," Lonnie said, abashed. "I'll call someone today, if there's time."

Nancy decided to follow up on Gaetan's comments about Etienne's financial worries. "Gaetan said that Etienne was worried about his job here—that the club was in financial trouble," she said. "Is that true?"

"Not at all," Lonnie scoffed. "Those underground parties are giving us some competition, and we've had some unusual expenses because of plumbing and wiring problems, but the business is rock solid."

"I recall Bess saying you had a problem with a water tank right before she was abducted."

"There was a problem with the valve," Lonnie explained. "But it's all fixed now."

"We'll be on our way and let you get back to work, Lonnie," Nancy said.

"You girls coming to the Halloween bash tonight?" he asked. They nodded. "Bess isn't coming back to work yet, I understand."

George started to reply, but Nancy cut her off. "She's been feeling a little under the weather since her ordeal, so she's not coming," she fibbed.

"That's too bad," Lonnie said. "See you two later, anyway."

"Why did you lie about Bess's not coming tonight?" George asked as they headed back to the car, which was parked along the street.

"I want to keep it as quiet as possible that Bess will be there," Nancy replied. "It doesn't hurt to take precautions." They arrived at the spot where the car was parked.

"What's that?" George exclaimed, pointing at Nancy's car.

Nancy looked at where George was pointing, and gasped. Someone had smashed a large granite rock down onto the hood of the car, denting it badly.

A piece of paper was fluttering underneath the rock. Nancy pulled out the paper and read it. "It's a note," she said, reading it out loud. "'Stay away from the Razor's Edge tonight—or you'll be the next to die!'"

Chapter

Twelve

WHO COULD HAVE left this note?" George wondered aloud. "They're threatening to kill you, Nancy."

"The person who left this note is probably the same one who murdered Etienne," Nancy replied. "And who helped kidnap Bess." One thing the note proved to Nancy—Gaetan couldn't be the guilty party.

"I'm going to call B.D. about this note right away," she said. "Let's get this stupid rock off my car."

Together, Nancy and George lifted the rock off the hood of the car and heaved it onto the sidewalk. Nancy surveyed the damage—the hood was dented and scratched, but the car was still driveable. "The fact that whoever left this note used a granite rock reminds me of our friend at the granite quarry, Tom Kragen," Nancy said, remembering the suspicious rockslide and Tom's veiled threat to her earlier in the day. "Maybe he's warning me to stay off the case."

On the way home, Nancy and George stopped by the River Heights police station to show the note to B. D. Hawkins. The police detective was as puzzled by the note as Nancy was. "This certainly indicates that we have another active suspect on our hands—a potentially dangerous one," he declared.

Nancy described her suspicions regarding Tom Kragen, including her run-in with him earlier that day. She also described Lucas's odd behavior the day before.

B.D. rolled his eyes when Nancy described the doorman. "Are you talking about Lucas Diego, who works over at the Edge? Big guy, with a curly black beard?" Nancy nodded. "We've had dealings with him before." B.D. spun around in his swivel desk-seat to face a computer monitor and keyboard. He punched in Lucas's name. "See? This guy's a really bad dude. He's got a rap sheet a mile long."

Peering over the detective's shoulder at the

monitor, Nancy and George saw a list of arrests and convictions under Lucas's name. "He once served a sentence for assault with a deadly weapon," George whispered to Nancy.

B.D. was reading from the police file. "It says here he used to be an ambulance driver, if you can believe it. But he got busted for pilfering medical supplies."

"Medical supplies," Nancy echoed. Her eyes widened. "Like ether?"

B.D. snapped his fingers. "Yes! Lucas might have a supply of that kind of stuff on hand." He reached into his desk drawer and pulled out a bulky file. "I want to show you something else," B.D. said. He handed her a dog-eared leather day planner. "This was Etienne's daily schedule book," the detective explained. "We found it in the glove compartment of his car."

Nancy scanned the book, which was crammed with notations about Etienne's daily activities. "Look at the section for today—October Thirty-first," B.D. directed her.

Nancy turned the pages until she reached October 31. The section was empty except for a cryptic notation: E 2h.

"What do you make of that?" he asked.

Nancy thought for a moment. " *'E'* is the in crowd's nickname for the Edge," she said. "And

Etienne's French, so '2h' probably refers to two A.M."

"So he was planning to meet someone at the Edge at two A.M.," George commented.

Nancy stared at the notation in Etienne's day planner. "I'm sure this meeting was something significant," she said. "The club is closed before two A.M., so Etienne might have been up to something when he planned the appointment for that time. I'd like to wait at the club tonight after it closes to see if anyone turns up at two."

B.D. looked uncertain. "That's definitely unorthodox," he said, starting to object. Then he shrugged. "As long as you're admitted to the club while it's open, it can't be called breaking and entering. Just keep your head down and don't give yourself away if anything develops. I'll order extra patrol cars to keep an eye on the place, as well."

"What about Gaetan," Nancy said, handing back the day planner. "Are you changing your mind about him as a suspect in the murder and the kidnapping?"

"We never had any evidence on him with regard to the abduction," B.D. replied. "And so far all we have is circumstantial evidence in Etienne's murder—the threat that Gaetan left on the answering machine, plus the fact that Etienne owed him money. We can't hold him much longer without solid evidence."

Nancy thanked the detective. Then she stood up and glanced at her watch. "We'd better get home and change into our costumes, George," she said. "This is one Halloween party I definitely don't want to miss!"

By eight o'clock Nancy, George, and Bess were standing in line in front of the Razor's Edge. Nancy shifted her weight from one foot to the other, trying to get used to the unfamiliar feel of roller skates. She'd packed an extra pair of shoes in case she got tired of skating. George was practicing rope tricks with her lasso.

"Bess, your outfit is a smash," Nancy said, taking note of several admiring glances from guys who were standing nearby. "Too bad you couldn't wear it yourself."

"There's always next year," Bess said. "But, anyway, I don't mind being a woman of mystery in this ninja outfit of yours."

It was time to go in. Lucas was not at his post, Nancy noted. Some other doorman was taking his place.

Soon the Halloween bash was in full swing. It

was fun to stand around, taking in everyone's costumes. Nancy couldn't decide which was her favorite—each costume seemed more appealing than the next. She waved to a couple that she knew who were wearing his-and-her Tarzan and Jane outfits.

A new DJ had taken Etienne's place, Nancy observed. He played a slightly different mix of music—less appealing than Etienne's, but very danceable. A big crowd was already hitting the floor.

Nancy spotted Tom Kragen. He and a male friend were dressed as samurai warriors. Nancy kept an eye on Tom as the evening progressed. He obviously recognized Bess despite her costume, because he kept glancing in her direction. He did not try to engage her in conversation, though.

As she was heading to the ladies' room at one point, Nancy felt a hand tap her shoulder. She turned and saw someone wearing a Cleopatra costume with a glittering gold half-mask. "Nancy?" a girl's voice said hesitantly.

Nancy recognized the voice. It was Charity Freeborn. In the regal Egyptian queen's costume, Charity's looks were utterly transformed. She was glamorous. "Hi, Charity," Nancy said, greeting her.

Charity checked around her hesitantly. "I need to talk with you. Let's go where we won't be overheard." She led Nancy to a spot just outside Lonnie's office door. "I wanted to know what you'd heard about Gaetan's case," she said anxiously.

"The detective in charge said they may have to drop the charges unless they gather more evidence," Nancy explained.

Charity let out a huge sigh of relief. "Thank goodness," she said. "I've been so worried."

"Charity, have you given any more thought to going home?" Nancy asked gently. "It would be good to have your family's support at a time like this."

"I've talked to them on the phone," Charity said softly. "I may go see them soon."

"Good," Nancy replied. "I know they miss you."

"Thanks, Nancy. I'd better get going. I just stopped by to see who was making this scene tonight, but I'm glad I got a chance to talk with you." She turned and melted back into the crowd in the front lobby.

Nancy continued on to the ladies' room, where she changed her shoes. Glad to be on solid footing again, she decided to look for Lonnie, to talk to him about the case and about his door-man. Nancy stepped inside Lonnie's office and did a quick check of the place. Lonnie wasn't there. Nancy was about to leave when her eye fell on a bright pink notice that was lying partially hidden under a book on his desk. The paper said: OFFICIAL NOTICE—TERMS OF FORECLO-SURE. It was from a local bank, informing Lonnie that he had thirty days to pay an out-standing debt, or the club would be seized.

Nancy froze, astonished. How could this be? she wondered. Lonnie had lied about the club being in good financial health, when it was clear the opposite was true! Nancy resolved to con-front him with her new discovery.

Nancy asked the girl at the coat check where she might find Lonnie. The girl shrugged and pointed to the door that led to the dressing room and utility areas. Nancy went through the door and down the hallway, listening for the club owner.

Pausing outside the water tank room, which was beside the dressing room she'd been in the day before, Nancy heard a loud, ominous hissing noise coming from inside. She opened the door to see a tangled web of pipes running out from an old, rusty tank. A low, metallic gurgling was

emanating from one of the pipes. Nancy stood
uncertainly for a moment, wondering whether
she should call a maintenance person. At that
moment the pipe burst its seam. The rupture
released a deadly spray of boiling steam directly
toward Nancy's face!

Chapter

Thirteen

NANCY DOVE to the ground to avoid being hit by the blast of scalding white steam that the pipe had spewed forth. She lay there a moment, shaking, while the boiling vapors shot directly over her head. The room was rumbling and clanging with the sound of machinery under stress.

Lonnie Cavello rushed into the room. "What are you doing in here?" he sputtered. "This is not a safe area."

"You're telling *me,*" Nancy said, climbing to her feet. The spray of steam had stopped, for the moment. "I was looking for you when I heard some kind of mechanical clatter in here. That pipe blew out some steam that almost scalded me to death."

Lonnie managed to compose himself, but he still seemed upset. "Are you all right?" he finally said. Nancy nodded.

After grabbing a thick rag from a hook, Lonnie used it to twist shut a valve on the water tank. "This'll shut off the flow to that broken pipe," he explained. "Why were you looking for me?"

"When we were discussing the finances of the Razor's Edge a while back, you neglected to mention that the club is in foreclosure," Nancy said, watching his reaction.

Lonnie waved at her dismissively. "I didn't consider that any of your business," he answered stiffly. He wheeled around to face her. "Look, Nancy. I think your amateur investigation has gone far enough. The police have their suspect in Etienne's murder, and probably Bess's kidnapping as well. Why don't you leave it alone?"

Nancy was surprised by the vehemence in Lonnie's tone. "Because we don't know the whole story yet," she said flatly.

"Some things are better left unknown," Lonnie said, giving the valve a final twist. "Let the police handle it. And now I'd appreciate it if you'd leave this area. As you can see, it's not safe."

Nancy returned to the dance floor, her

thoughts churning over her encounter with Lonnie. Not only had he lied to her, but he told her to drop the case! Nancy wondered if he might be covering for Lucas in some way—or perhaps he had something of his own to hide.

A break in the music just then gave everyone a chance to mill around and talk.

Nancy's attention was directed to a commotion going on in one corner of the room, near the exit door where Bess had disappeared. Coming closer, she saw Bess and George engaged in a heated discussion with Tom Kragen and his friend. Bess had removed her mask, and her blue eyes were glittering with anger.

"How *dare* you say that about me, Tom Kragen!" Nancy heard her say.

Nancy pushed her way between Bess and George and the two guys. "What's going on here?" she demanded.

"A friend of mine told me that Tom is still spreading that story that he and I are going out," Bess fumed. "And I want him to stop!"

Tom seemed abashed. "I guess it was a little white lie," he admitted.

"That's a cop-out, Tom, and you know it," Bess retorted. "Lies aren't so little when they affect somebody else."

Tom took a step back. "Sorry, Bess," he mumbled. "I won't do it again." He and his friend turned and retreated toward the front exit.

"What a jerk," George said after Tom had left.

"I'm going to follow him and see where he goes," Nancy said, turning to head for the exit. "Keep an eye on things at the club for me until I get back."

As Nancy dashed out the front door of the club, she spotted Tom and his friend climbing into a shiny new four-wheel-drive truck, which was parked in a small lot across the street. She hurried to her own car, which was parked at the curb. Nancy pulled out just in time to see Tom turning left onto the main drag.

Tom's truck was several car lengths ahead of Nancy's car as he maneuvered through traffic. At one intersection, he sped through a light just as it turned red. Nancy was blocked by the cars that were stopped ahead of her.

Nancy muttered to herself. She considered continuing her pursuit of Tom, then decided against it. She was beginning to worry about having left Bess and George back at the club. She turned around and drove back to the Edge.

It was almost midnight, and the Halloween party was beginning to wind down. Nancy found

Bess and George near the DJ's booth, talking to a couple of cute guys. She tapped Bess on the shoulder.

"I really hate to drag you away, but we need to talk," Nancy said. "Let's go to the dressing room."

After making sure they weren't being observed, Nancy led them through the lobby and down the tiled hallway to the dressing room. "What was Tom up to after he left?" Bess wanted to know.

Nancy shrugged. "I lost him in traffic, unfortunately. But if he's our man, I have a hunch he'll be back tonight at two A.M. But right now, frankly, I'm more suspicious of Lucas and Lonnie."

"Lonnie? And Lucas the doorman?" George gasped. "What would be their angle on the kidnapping, and Etienne's death?"

"That's what I'm hoping to find out tonight," Nancy replied.

"What should we do right now?" Bess asked.

"We need to hide out in the club somewhere until it closes," Nancy said. "Etienne had a notation in his day planner that he was going to meet someone here at two A.M. I want to see who keeps that appointment."

"What if no one shows?" George asked.

"I'm betting that someone will," Nancy replied.

"This would be a good place to hide," Bess said. "I don't think anyone ever comes in here."

"Good idea," Nancy said. The girls tucked themselves into various corners of the room, clicked off the light, and waited for two A.M. to roll around.

"I think I have to go to the bathroom," Bess whispered plaintively. Pressing the light on her wristwatch, Nancy saw that it was one-twenty A.M.

"Great timing, Bess," George groaned.

The three friends had been hiding in the dressing room for almost two hours. Nancy's neck was beginning to get stiff and sore, and she longed to stretch her limbs. "Just a little while longer, Bess," she whispered. "If no one shows up, we'll get out."

The minutes felt as if they were stretching into hours. Nancy checked her watch again—it was two A.M. There wasn't a hint of a sound or movement anywhere.

A few more long, tense minutes passed. Just as Nancy began to think that her hunch was wrong, they heard the sharp clang of metal crunching metal. The sound was coming from the room next door.

Running her hands along the connecting wall, Nancy groped around for the latched access window she'd seen earlier. She slid back the latch and opened the window a tiny crack.

Light flowed through the crack from the brightly lit room next door. Peering through the window, Nancy could see Lonnie Cavello and Lucas the doorman. The two men were fiddling with a valve on the water tank.

"Are you sure this is going to work, Lonnie?" Lucas was asking the club owner.

Lonnie shook his head impatiently. "Of course it's going to work," he said, holding a wrench on the valve. "I've managed to damage the water tank's safety valve in a way that will look totally accidental. When enough pressure builds up in the tank later tonight, this place will blow like the Fourth of July."

"And then you'll split the insurance money with me, right?" Lucas looked anxious.

"Of course, of course." Lonnie waved an impatient hand at the doorman. "With Etienne out of the picture, there'll be plenty left to split."

Nancy sat back, her heart thumping like mad. She tried to digest what she'd just overheard. The conversation between the two men made it perfectly clear—Lonnie and Lucas were getting ready to blow up the Razor's Edge for the insurance money!

Chapter

Fourteen

GEORGE AND BESS huddled around Nancy's shoulders, trying to figure out what was happening. "This sounds bad," George whispered. "Can they possibly blow up the club like they say?"

"Yes, I'm afraid so," Nancy replied.

"Oh, Nancy!" Bess's blue eyes went round with fear. "What'll we do?"

Nancy was thinking fast. "While they're busy working in the pump room, I think you two should get out of the club and contact the police. B.D. told me he'd keep extra patrol cars in the vicinity. I'll stay here and try to figure out what to do about Lonnie and Lucas."

"Are you sure, Nan?" George asked anxiously.

"I don't like the idea of leaving you here by yourself."

Nancy looked through the window crack again. Lucas had disappeared. "I'll be fine," she said swiftly. "Hurry now, before Lonnie comes out. And watch out for Lucas. He's skulking somewhere around here." George and Bess slipped silently from the dressing room.

Lonnie was absorbed in putting the finishing touches on the valve work. Those finishing touches, Nancy knew, would soon spark a massive explosion that would destroy the building they were standing in.

Nancy knew she didn't have much time. Worried that Bess and George might not locate the patrol car, she decided to risk leaving the dressing room to call B. D. Hawkins from Lonnie's office. She crept from the dressing room and tiptoed down the hall toward the lobby. She strode across the carpeted floor to Lonnie's office.

Nancy picked up the phone and dialed 911. When the police dispatcher answered, Nancy opened her mouth to report an emergency. Before she could utter a word, she felt a sharp blow across the back of her neck. Then everything went black!

* * *

When Nancy woke up, she felt rough ropes cutting into her wrists and ankles. She was lying on the floor of the dressing room next to Bess and George, who were also tied up.

"Nancy, I'm so glad to see you wake up." George sounded relieved. "Bess and I were afraid they'd really injured you."

Nancy shook her head to clear the bright spots that were swimming in front of her eyes. "What happened, George?" she asked weakly.

"Bess and I got delayed when we tried to get out of the club because there was a chain fastened to the front door," George explained. "When we tried to sneak out the back exit, Lucas heard us."

"Yeah, that big oaf." Bess spat out the words. "When he brought us back to the dressing room, we saw you lying on the floor."

"I was trying to get through to the police," Nancy said, rubbing her head. "But I didn't get a chance to tell them what was going on."

Lonnie Cavello, flanked by Lucas, entered the dressing room. "I see you're finally awake, Nancy," he observed. Then he sighed. "It probably would have been easier if you had just stayed unconscious, when you consider what's in store for you."

"What's in store for us, Lonnie?" Nancy asked boldly. "Blowing up your club?"

"With you in it, my dear." Lonnie's words sent a chill creeping up Nancy's spine. She had no doubt that he meant what he said. There was an unsettling deadness of expression in his eyes.

Nancy knew she had to stall for time. "Are you blowing it up for the insurance money?" she asked. She cast covert glances about the room, looking for anything she might use to escape.

Lonnie caught her glance. "Forget it, Nancy. There's no way you're going to escape. You and your meddling friends will be the unfortunate victims of a tragic commercial accident. I'd be surprised if they even manage to identify your bodies."

Nancy could hear Bess moan softly in the corner of the room. "How about Etienne?" she asked. "Was he an 'unfortunate victim' as well?"

Lonnie's face twisted into a ghastly smile. "Etienne was not entirely innocent, as you might have guessed. He helped me devise this plan to blow up the club in a way that insurance investigators would not suspect as sabotage. He was pretty hard up for money, and he thought this would be an easy way to score some major cash."

"Was he in on the plot to kidnap Bess, as well?" Nancy asked.

Lonnie nodded. "Bess stumbled into the room with the water heater and caught me talking with

Lucas about our plot, so I ordered Etienne to cut the power and Lucas to knock her out with some ether and take her to my house."

"I had no idea what you were doing," Bess said, shocked. "There was no need for anything like that."

"I didn't want to take any chances, Bess," Lonnie said. "But I realize now that I panicked unnecessarily on that one. While I was debating how to get rid of you, Etienne came over to my house and argued that you couldn't have seen anything and should be let go. I guess he had a change of heart when he realized someone might get hurt. I refused, but he came back and sneaked you out and let you go on his own."

"So Etienne must have released Bess after he left George and me at the amusement park," Nancy said. "That's why he was in such a hurry. He knew that George and I were heading back to the Razor's Edge, and he wanted to get there first, with Bess."

"Exactly," Lonnie said. "After that, Etienne started having second thoughts about our entire plan to blow up the club."

"So you killed him." George's voice rose with anger.

"I'm afraid so," Lonnie said. "I took care of

him myself. Just like I'm going to get rid of the three of you."

Nancy interrupted him. "What about after Bess was released," she asked. "Was that you who tried to break into her house?"

"No, that was me!" Lucas admitted.

Lonnie nodded. "My loyal doorman felt so bad about letting Bess get away that he tried to fetch her back. Once again, however, you thwarted our plans, Nancy."

Lonnie chuckled. "I admire your courage. It's truly a pity you have to die."

Lonnie turned and left the dressing room, with Lucas dogging his heels. Nancy heard them get to work in the room next door. Then Lonnie stuck his head through the access window. "And in case you're wondering, Nancy, we've turned up the water pressure to maximum capacity. Enjoy your last thirty minutes."

Half an hour! That didn't give them much time. Nancy heard Lonnie and Lucas leave. She wriggled and flopped her way across the floor until she reached the spot where George was lying. "George, do you still carry around your penknife key chain?" she asked.

"Sure do," George replied. "It's in the back pocket of my jeans."

"Swing around until your back is pressed against mine, George," Nancy directed her. "I'm going to try to get the knife out."

George twisted around until she and Nancy were sitting awkwardly back to back. Nancy put her hands into George's pocket, grasped the penknife, and gradually slid it out. She had to move slowly to avoid dropping the knife. Finally she pulled it free. "I'm going to put the knife in your hand and open it, George," she explained. "Then I'll rub the rope against the blade until it breaks."

George caught the knife in her hand and held it while Nancy pried it open with her fingernail. Then she put the knotted rope against the blade and started rubbing it back and forth. The rope began to fray.

"How much time do you think has passed?" Bess asked anxiously. "Lonnie said we had only thirty minutes."

"Too much time, I'm afraid," Nancy replied tensely. They could hear a gurgling sound coming from the room next door, followed by an even more ominous rumbling. Nancy doubled her efforts to cut the rope. She winced as the blade slipped at one point, cutting into her skin.

With a final push against the knife, the rope

suddenly fell apart. Nancy hurriedly untied her feet, then freed George and Bess.

The rumbling sound from the room next door had become a frightening, high-pitched squeal, as if thousands of pounds of water pressure were straining to rip loose.

"No time to try to stop it. Let's get out of here," Nancy shouted. She, George, and Bess scrambled down the hall, through the lobby, across the dance floor and out the rear exit into the alley. Bess stumbled, skinning her knee. Nancy and George helped her to her feet, then they continued running to the end of the alley.

Now the rumbling sound could be heard outside too. Nancy glanced over her shoulder just in time to see a huge fireball rip through the building. The Edge was exploding!

Chapter

Fifteen

"Get down!" Nancy shouted. The three dove for cover behind a Dumpster as a shower of debris, including shards of glass, rained down on them. Nancy glanced at her friends—like her, they were frightened, but unhurt.

Smoke from the fireball rose into an oily cloud above the site of the explosion. Sirens were already wailing in the distance as they rose slowly to their feet.

"Here come the squad cars and fire engines," Nancy cried. "Stay here and wait for them," she called back to the other two. "I'm going after Lonnie."

Nancy raced around the block to her car. She

opened the door and rummaged in her glove compartment until she found the paper where she'd written down Lonnie's address.

In an expensive residential neighborhood in a newer part of town, Nancy found Lonnie's house. She parked at the curb outside it and spent a few minutes observing. All appeared quiet. Nancy couldn't see Lonnie, though. She hopped out of her car to move up to the house to make sure he was inside before she went to call the police.

Moving slowly from window to window, she peered inside for even a glimpse of him. Nothing.

At the back door, which had been left ajar, she decided to enter and risk confronting him. At least she could use the phone to call 911. Nancy picked up the wall phone and made a whispered emergency call to the police.

She winced as she heard a sound behind her in the kitchen. "So we meet again, Nancy," Lonnie announced. Nancy turned around. The club owner held a gun in his hand, and he was pointing it right at Nancy! "I don't know how you escaped that explosion, but you were stupid to come here," he said. "Now you're going to die on the spot." He leveled the gun directly at her chest.

Using the telephone wire like a tether, Nancy

145

hurled the receiver at Lonnie's head. The phone glanced off his brow, stunning him for a moment. Nancy followed this up with a powerful karate chop to his neck. Lonnie sunk to the floor like a stone, out cold.

Nancy could hear patrol cars pulling up to the curb outside Lonnie's home. She calmly walked out the front door to greet them.

"Nancy!" Bess, who had ridden in B. D. Hawkins's car with George, ran up to Nancy and threw her arms around her. "We were talking to B.D. in his cruiser when the dispatcher relayed your call. I was afraid Lonnie had done something awful to you."

"It looks like Lonnie got his lights knocked out," B.D. called out from the kitchen. The girls joined him there. "It's only fitting, considering what he's been dishing out recently," he finished.

"What about Lucas?" Nancy asked. "Is he still at large?"

George walked Nancy back into the living room and pointed out the window to the third in the line of squad cars parked outside Lonnie's home under a streetlight. The bearded doorman was handcuffed in the backseat. "They caught him a few blocks away from the explosion," George explained.

"Yeah, he suddenly doesn't look so scary when he's locked in a squad car!" Bess chimed in.

The next evening Nancy invited Bess and George to have dinner at her house. "B.D. called me a little while ago," Nancy told them as she served salad. "It turns out that Lonnie Cavello's name isn't even Lonnie Cavello. It's Howard Snell—and he's wanted in three states for insurance fraud."

"Well, one thing is certain. This Howard-turned-Lonnie's criminal career has come to an end," George said, popping a crouton into her mouth.

From his spot at the head of the table, Carson Drew smiled at his daughter. "And Gaetan has been released, thank goodness," he said. "I hate more than anything to see an innocent man put in jail for something he didn't do."

"Did I tell you that Tom Kragen called me to apologize for coming on so strong?" Bess asked Nancy. "He said he was sorry."

"Yes, Bess, I heard about that from George," Nancy said with a grin. "I guess he was just struck with an innocent case of puppy love."

"Yeah, Bess, it must be tough to be so admired," George said wryly.

"And it goes to show that the landslide at the quarry really was an accident. I had my doubts at the time," Nancy commented.

Just then Nancy's front doorbell rang. She rose to answer it. Gaetan and Charity were standing on the front porch. They broke into broad smiles when they spotted Nancy.

"Gaetan! I'm glad to see you," Nancy said, welcoming them. "I understand they released you as soon as it was clear that Lonnie and Lucas were the real culprits in Etienne's murder and Bess's kidnapping."

Gaetan was pleased. "Yes, and your father is representing me in my immigration case. It seems as if there will be no problem about my staying in this country, after all."

"And Gaetan already has a couple of musician's jobs lined up," Charity said happily.

"Are you and your family back together?" Nancy asked.

Charity nodded. "We made a deal. They'll welcome Gaetan into our family *if* we agree to put off getting married for a few more years." Nancy thought that for the first time since she'd met her, Charity seemed relaxed and happy, completely different from the hotheaded teen she'd first encountered.

"Putting off marriage awhile doesn't sound

unfair," Nancy commented. "There's plenty of time for that in the future."

Charity positively glowed. "Yes, and thanks to you, Nancy, Gaetan and I *have* a future," she said. "We just wanted to come by and thank you in person. And to apologize for my horrible behavior at the amusement park. I don't know what came over me—I was so choked up with anger at my father's attitude toward Gaetan. I hope I can make it up to you by inviting you, Bess, and George to a little get-together at my house later tonight. Kind of a welcome-home party I'm throwing for myself."

"By 'little get-together,' Charity means at least one hundred people," Gaetan joked. "And that's not including our friends from the dance parties."

Nancy was ecstatic that things had worked out so well for Charity and Gaetan. "We'll be the first ones to arrive," she promised happily.

Nancy's next case:

Nancy's spending Thanksgiving in Paris, the city of light, love . . . and mystery. Her neighbor is Ellen Mathieson, a professor whose study of painter Josephine Solo has suddenly taken a dark and disturbing turn. Ellen's research assistant is dead—killed in an accident exactly like the one that took Solo's life six months before!

Josephine Solo left a legacy of secrecy and scandal . . . even the possibility of a double life. But Nancy begins to suspect that some of the professor's students also have something to hide. Paris is full of powerful temptations—forbidden romance, secret passions, financial greed—any one of which could lead to a motive for murder . . . in *The Picture of Guilt,* Case #101 in The Nancy Drew Files™.

THE HARDY BOYS® CASEFILES

☐ #1: DEAD ON TARGET	73992-1/$3.99	☐ #57: TERROR ON TRACK 73093-2/$3.99
☐ #2: EVIL, INC.	73668-X/$3.75	☐ #60: DEADFALL 73096-7/$3.99
☐ #3: CULT OF CRIME	68263-3/$3.75	☐ #61: GRAVE DANGER 73097-5/$3.99
☐ #4: THE LAZARUS PLOT	73995-6/$3.75	☐ #62: FINAL GAMBIT 73098-3/$3.75
☐ #5: EDGE OF DESTRUCTION	73669-8/$3.99	☐ #63: COLD SWEAT 73099-1/$3.75
☐ #6: THE CROWNING OF	73670-1/$3.50	☐ #64: ENDANGERED SPECIES 73100-9/$3.99
TERROR		☐ #65: NO MERCY 73101-7/$3.99
☐ #7: DEATHGAME	73672-8/$3.99	☐ #66: THE PHOENIX EQUATION 73102-5/$3.99
☐ #8: SEE NO EVIL	73673-6/$3.50	☐ #67: LETHAL CARGO 73103-3/$3.75
☐ #9: THE GENIUS THIEVES	73674-4/$3.50	☐ #68: ROUGH RIDING 73104-1/$3.75
☐ #12: PERFECT GETAWAY	73675-2/$3.50	☐ #69: MAYHEM IN MOTION 73105-X/$3.75
☐ #13: THE BORGIA DAGGER	73676-0/$3.50	☐ #70: RIGGED FOR REVENGE 73106-8/$3.75
☐ #14: TOO MANY TRAITORS	73677-9/$3.50	☐ #71: REAL HORROR 73107-6/$3.99
☐ #29: THICK AS THIEVES	74663-4/$3.50	☐ #72: SCREAMERS 73108-4/$3.75
☐ #30: THE DEADLIEST DARE	74613-8/$3.50	☐ #73: BAD RAP 73109-2/$3.99
☐ #32: BLOOD MONEY	74665-0/$3.50	☐ #74: ROAD PIRATES 73110-6/$3.99
☐ #33: COLLISION COURSE	74666-9/$3.50	☐ #75: NO WAY OUT 73111-4/$3.99
☐ #35: THE DEAD SEASON	74105-5/$3.50	☐ #76: TAGGED FOR TERROR 73112-2/$3.99
☐ #37: DANGER ZONE	73751-1/$3.75	☐ #77: SURVIVAL RUN 79461-2/$3.99
☐ #41: HIGHWAY ROBBERY	70038-3/$3.75	☐ #78: THE PACIFIC CONSPIRACY 79462-0/$3.99
☐ #42: THE LAST LAUGH	74614-6/$3.50	☐ #79: DANGER UNLIMITED 79463-9/$3.99
☐ #44: CASTLE FEAR	74615-4/$3.75	☐ #80: DEAD OF NIGHT 79464-7/$3.99
☐ #45: IN SELF-DEFENSE	70042-1/$3.75	☐ #81: SHEER TERROR 79465-5/$3.99
☐ #46: FOUL PLAY	70043-X/$3.75	☐ #82: POISONED PARADISE 79466-3/$3.99
☐ #47: FLIGHT INTO DANGER	70044-8/$3.99	☐ #83: TOXIC REVENGE 79467-1/$3.99
☐ #48: ROCK 'N' REVENGE	70045-6/$3.50	☐ #84: FALSE ALARM 79468-X/$3.99
☐ #49: DIRTY DEEDS	70046-4/$3.99	☐ #85: WINNER TAKE ALL 79469-8/$3.99
☐ #50: POWER PLAY	70047-2/$3.99	☐ #86: VIRTUAL VILLAINY 79470-1/$3.99
☐ #52: UNCIVIL WAR	70049-9/$3.50	☐ #87: DEADMAN IN DEADWOOD 79471-X/$3.99
☐ #53: WEB OF HORROR	73089-4/$3.99	☐ #88: INFERNO OF FEAR 79472-8/$3.99
☐ #54: DEEP TROUBLE	73090-8/$3.99	☐ #89: DARKNESS FALLS 79473-6/$3.99
☐ #55: BEYOND THE LAW	73091-6/$3.50	☐ #90: DEADLY ENGAGEMENT 79474-4/$3.99
☐ #56: HEIGHT OF DANGER	73092-4/$3.50	☐ #91: HOT WHEELS 79475-2/$3.99
		☐ #92: SABOTAGE AT SEA 79476-0/$3.99

HAVE YOU SEEN THE NANCY DREW® FILES™ LATELY?